DATE			

UNEASY
LIES
THE
HEAD

Also by Robert Tine

STATE OF GRACE

ROBERT TINE

UNEASY
LIES
THE
HEAD

THE VIKING PRESS • NEW YORK

Copyright © 1982 by Robert Tine
All rights reserved
First published in 1982 by The Viking Press
625 Madison Avenue, New York, N.Y. 10022
Published simultaneously in Canada by
Penguin Books Canada Limited

LIBRARY OF CONGRESS CATALOGING IN PUBLICATION DATA
Tine, Robert.
Uneasy lies the head.
I. Title.
PS3570.I48U5   813'.54   81-65283
ISBN 0-670-74067-5   AACR2

Printed in the United States of America
Set in Baskerville

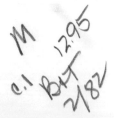

For Mara, with love

UNEASY
LIES
THE
HEAD

Letter to the Editor, *The Times*
6 October 198-

Sir,
Having read with interest the debate in these columns over the efficacy of the monarchy in the modern age, I would advise those who consider it an expensive anachronism to give heed to the words of Viscount Bryce: "The value of the Crown lies not in the power it wields, but in the power it denies to those who would abuse it."

I am, etc.,

Noah Sinclair, OM

PROLOGUE

There was not enough light under the darkened theater marquee for the few passersby to see the blue-black welt on Brenda Pomeroy's cheekbone. She had tried to hide it as best she could with a layer of rose-colored makeup, but it still showed, tinting the arc underneath her eye an angry purple.

Mac had done it to her. He was on the phone at the time: she had brought in her take for the night before, £70—not bad considering the weather—but he had said it wasn't enough and hit her, quite unexpectedly, with the shaft of the telephone receiver. He did it, he'd said, so she'd show more initiative in future.

She was scared. For hours she had cruised Shaftesbury Avenue and so far had come up almost empty. A few kids from some polytechnic had led her on, but they had only been joking. She had heard them laughing as they walked away from her, coarse unformed adolescent voices echoing in the empty street. The next day at school they'd laugh again when they told their mates how they put one over on a tart. An old guy had agreed to her price—£15—but had scarpered when they got to her place. He gave her £5 and said he was sorry. If she brought Mac five quid he'd kill her.

She had parked herself in front of the late-night strip joints, hoping to harness the lust of the men who staggered out. But nothing. Too sick from watery drinks and thump-thump music, they lurched by, not even noticing her. One by one the signs were turned off, leaving her the empty streets, a booby prize that she shared with a tramp or two. If things got much worse, she would have to head for the docks, to see if she could scare up a little business. But that was dangerous. Brenda could feel the sharp tears of desperation coming on.

It was cold and damp, and to keep herself warm she teetered from side to side on platform shoes so thick-soled that she looked as if her feet were buckled to weights. Over her tight T-shirt and her tighter shorts she wore a cardigan sweater, a garment not designed to allure, but she was so bloody cold. She had buried her hands in the pockets, stretching the sweater down from her shoulders almost to her thighs; it made her look thinner, just as her lank, straight, dark-brown hair made her face seem paler. The coroner would later establish her age at seventeen years.

She scanned the empty street. Far away, almost at the corner of Charing Cross Road, a man, and, she could tell by his walk, a possibility, came toward her. He was far enough away that he couldn't see the bruise, so she stepped from under the marquee into the light, available. He saw her and crossed the street toward her.

As he neared, her heart sank: he didn't look the type. He slowed his pace but that didn't mean anything; everyone slows down to sneak a look at a whore. She fought panic. This was her last chance of the night, she could feel it. As he passed she abandoned her usual "After a lark, love?" and said quietly, "I'll do anything, mister, *anything.*"

She was perfect. Young, scared, a bit stupid, set up in a greasy little bed-sitter above a tobacconist on Frith Street. Her little whore's getup, the platform shoes and shorts, was pathetic, guaranteed to inspire a certain sympathy among the readers of the prole papers, the widely read, working-class *Sketch,* the

4

Daily Mirror, and the *Sun.* Her room was like a stage set: lumpy bed, anonymous quilted vinyl armchair, grayed curtains, a photograph of a film star cut neatly from a magazine and pinned over the bed. Perfect.

She stood in front of the metal gas grate. "Got fifty p for the gas?" she said, rubbing her bare arms. "I'm freezing."

With the return of her circulation came her patter. "What were you doing out so late? Couldn't sleep?" She spoke in flat Midland tones. "Hope you're not sleepy now." She winked.

He gave her a coin to put in the gas meter.

" 'Ere, take off your coat."

The gas heater in the cracked fireplace glowed. He stood awkwardly.

"Your coat," she repeated.

"I'll leave it on."

She gave him a "suit yourself" look. "Shy? I'll go first." She wriggled out of her T-shirt, exposing her tiny breasts and the fresh spray of acne above them.

"I'm freezing all over." She giggled and turned to face the heat.

As she bent to absorb its warmth she heard him move to stand behind her. A hand passed over her shoulder and moved around under her chin. She felt the coarse weave of the man's coat on her skin and she moved back against him, rubbing like a cat.

"From behind?" she asked, giggling.

The hand paused for a moment on her chin and then, quickly, closed over her mouth and nostrils. Brenda started violently, her eyes wide. A strong arm, his right, snaked under her chin and with a curt, tight squeeze and a wrench, broke Brenda Pomeroy's neck.

CHAPTER ONE

As the massed band of the Brigade of Guards marched under Admiralty Arch, they struck up a sprightly martial air and strode smartly down The Mall. Just behind them were the Royal Hussars, led by their Colonel-in-Chief, HRH Prince Victor Edward, the King's brother and, not that it mattered, heir to the throne. It did not matter because Britain had a new king, crowned and anointed not twenty-five minutes earlier in Westminster Abbey. Victor Edward, the Duke of Moreland, "Snuffy" as he was known to his contemporaries at Sandhurst, shakoed and cuirassed and mounted on a roan gelding of extraordinary size, was pleased that the show was almost over and immensely relieved to be out of church. All that remained for him to do was wave a bit from the balcony of Buckingham Palace and then hop it back to Hampshire. He hated being in London.

Snaking behind him for a mile or two, all the way back to Westminster Abbey, was the coronation procession. Somewhere in the middle of it all, sitting in the gold state coach, was his brother, Gordie. King George VII was, without doubt, beloved. That morning in *The Times* the editorial had pointed out that he was "the brightest spot in Britain's bleak landscape." He was also, by anyone's reckoning, the world's most eligible bachelor.

A dense crowd, dozens deep and backed all the way to the base of Carlton Terrace, had lined The Mall, the stately approach to Buckingham Palace. Many of the onlookers had stood there since early that morning, some since the night before, sleeping in St. James's Park. Now they put away their thermos flasks and packets of sandwiches and the gossip and bonhomie exchanged between strangers to watch the coronation procession. Young children clutching plastic Union Jacks sat on daddies' aching shoulders, arched-necked schoolboys, pensioners—the men with medals on their breasts, the women in floral hats, looking like carbon copies of the former Queen Mother—and teenagers with permanent sneers pressed into their faces, stared at the color and the pomp of Coronation Day, and cheered.

Many of the older folk watching the procession of gold and scarlet narrowed their eyes a bit and remembered: when there had been no VAT, when the map had been all one color, when Suez had been a British company town instead of a national humiliation, when British ships carried British goods to a British east; before Asians from Africa and Africans from the West Indies moved in and called themselves British; before men in Essen and Stuttgart and Osaka had carted off the money and pride that had been Britain's alone; when British-made meant better-made, and it had been British—not American—"know-how"; and the little boats, the blitz, El Alamein, fine hours now dog-eared and discolored like old photographs. Watching the procession and listening to the music, it was possible, just for a second, to snatch back the past and be proud again. Only the very young and the foreign tourists gaped as if at Disneyland.

"Harriet, look at that!"

"This must have cost a bundle!"

Detective Inspector Sam "Smudge" Huddleston, standing at the base of The Mall, remembered, and was proud. A small man, not short exactly, but not tall either, he straightened his spine and pulled his shoulders back, adding an inch or two to his height, as Prince Victor Edward passed. He saluted silently and thought, Nice-looking fellow. A family man, the papers said.

Virtually every man on the police force was out that day, keeping an eye open, uniforms and plainclothes alike, doing their best to see that nothing marred the coronation. The IRA was expected to make an appearance as was a militant Welsh group with an unpronounceable name consisting mostly of consonants. Some right-wingers had threatened a show of force, and some Trotskyites had threatened to retaliate. Loonies, Huddleston called them.

He was an old-fashioned "What's all this, then?" copper. He had spent half his career in uniform, pounding various pavements in the West End, a helpful, courteous bobby whom shopkeepers were fond of and to whom elderly American tourists, after getting directions to Buckingham Palace and taking his photograph, would extend invitations: "If you're ever in Chicago, Officer . . ."

Smudge Huddleston counted his years on the beat as the most important part of his training. "Taught me about people," he was fond of saying. Although he had been in plainclothes for fifteen years—ten of them investigating murders—he still felt as if he wore the uniform. For others, notably criminals, he may as well have; even the least-experienced hoodlum instantly recognized Smudge Huddleston as Old Bill, a copper. It might have been his thick-soled shoes ("Look after your feet," he'd solemnly inform new recruits; "your feet are your best friends") or perhaps his slightly stooped walk and the dirty-brown walrus mustache, or the ponderous ruminating tone of voice—no one could say exactly—but the sum of the parts added up to a neat total: Huddleston just *looked* like a policeman. As Detective Superintendent Alf Hartley, Huddleston's superior, put it, "You could dress Smudge in a toga or a ballet tutu and he'd still look like a bleeding copper."

Well, to Huddleston's way of thinking, that wasn't such a bad thing. As he grew older—and his retirement was just over a year away—he viewed with more and more distaste the new breed of policeman. The younger blokes in the Criminal Investigation Department—some of them Huddleston's superiors—were, in his view, more like pop stars than policemen. They might be tough but they dressed a bit flashy for his taste and had carefully coiffed hair that they fussed with continually. Huddleston wore his short, back and sides, like a badge.

"Very Carnaby Street," Smudge would observe to some of the old-timers like Alf Hartley. "Very mod, Chelsea boots and the like . . ." Huddleston's vocabulary was always about twenty years behind the times. Until relatively recently juvenile delinquents had still been "teddy boys" and petty thieves "skivs."

"In a world of his own, bless him," said Alf Hartley, laughing, when the younger men complained that Smudge was an embarrassment. But Smudge hadn't got far to go before the paddock, and the older men were determined to let him down easy—Huddleston had always played fair and, more important, had played with the team. His colleagues weren't going to forget that now. Privately, Huddleston's juniors referred to working with him as "granddad duty" and had him type their reports. Smudge was an excellent typist.

The procession continued. A brigade of Royal Marines passed, and then the pipes of the Argylls, led by a massive pipes major waving an equally bulky silver-topped baton to the beat of a Scottish air Huddleston didn't recognize. A brace of RAF fighter planes raced overhead, temporarily drowning out the music; from Green Park came the rumblings of a salute fired by a battery of Royal Artillery.

Huddleston noticed a young man standing next to him, staring into the procession and beyond. His hair was a pleasant mauve color, his eyes were obscured by black wraparound sunglasses. He was about sixteen. The sharp edge of some PCP sprinkled on a Rothmans smoked a few minutes earlier was beginning to scythe through his brain.

"That's forty-two guns," said Smudge. "Only royalty gets a forty-two-gun salute." He smiled at the boy and wondered why his hair was such an odd color.

The boy looked up at Smudge through the heavily tinted glasses. Copper, he thought, and fought to look straight.

"Everyone else gets twenty-one guns," continued Smudge,

"doesn't matter who. The President of the U.S., the Prime Minister . . ."

"Yeah," said the kid, "right."

Smudge looked down The Mall. "His Majesty should be coming along any minute. I remember the last coronation—before you were born, most like . . ."

Fucking copper, fucking copper, fucking copper, the kid thought. His knees trembled.

"That was a day," said Smudge. "June 1953 . . . I remember it like yesterday. Pelting rain . . ." He looked down at his new friend to find him gone. A purple head bobbed unsteadily through the crowd down The Mall. Smudge watched him bump his way along. Just like his own son, Rodney, and all young people today, he thought. No sense of history. Only interested in themselves and the Beatles.

They were not being discreet.

Tony Pidgeon stared at the two young men as they scrabbled at the lock of the Jaguar parked in Queen Anne's Gate. Some people, thought Tony, are so bloody stupid. The two kids yelled instructions at one another angrily.

"Twist the bugger in the lock," said the larger of the two. His companion wrestled with a claw-toothed jimmy, trying to pull the whole lock from the door and scratching the smooth black paintwork in the process. Then he leaned on the handle of the tool, putting all his weight on it. Abruptly the tooth broke off in the lock.

"Fuck," he said.

"Fuck," said the other, staring at the door handle in fury. Someone had told them it would be easy. Tony Pidgeon—Detective Sergeant Tony Pidgeon, Scotland Yard—could just imagine the line some old con in Battersea had fed these two: "Nip up to the West End—everybody at the coronation—stick your jimmy in the lock. Bob's yer uncle—got yourself a Jag. . . ." He'd probably charged them twenty quid for the jimmy.

"Gimme that," said one of the thieves, whipping the heavy

10

handle from his companion's hand and smashing the window on the driver's side. He looked around to see if anyone had heard and saw Pidgeon.

"Fuck," said the window smasher.

Tony took a few steps toward them. "We were having a lovely coronation till you lot showed up," he said.

The two boys faced him, scared, but eager for a punch-up—two on one—so great was their frustration at being foiled by the Jaguar.

"You a copper?"

"That's right," said Pidgeon.

"Christ, Barry," said the one who hadn't broken the window.

"Shut up," said Barry. "You going to take us in, copper?"

Piegeon took one step closer and stuck his hands in his pockets. "Well, Barry," he said, "that depends."

"Yeah?" He waved the jimmy handle. "On what?"

"On how much I come to hate you in the next few minutes."

"What happens if you fall in love with us?" Barry sneered.

"I'll take you in." The threat rolled easily off his tongue. From The Mall just across the park came the sounds of the coronation procession like those of a far-off fair.

Tony Pidgeon had already mapped out the forthcoming fight in his mind. The big one, Barry, would swing with the handle—he'd be anxious to take Pidgeon out with one blow, so there would be a lot of force behind it. This would throw him off-balance and there would be ample time for Pidgeon to kick his balls in. The other one—he was almost pissing himself with fear, Pidgeon noticed—would be watching Barry, and could be dealt with easily.

"Going to beat us up, then?" Barry showed a set of well-cared-for National Health teeth and, without waiting for a reply, swung the jimmy at Pidgeon. The rather too-well-polished toe of Pidgeon's boot bisected the arc of Barry's wild swing and buried itself in the boy's crotch. Barry opened his mouth to scream but gasped for breath instead. He sank to the cobblestones.

Pidgeon started to throw a right at the other kid, who

11

squeaked and turned a shoulder to deflect the blow. Pidgeon stopped himself. Poor bloody sod, it was too damn easy. He grabbed the boy roughly by the shoulders.

"Take your playmate and hop it," he said.

"Police brutality," said the boy timidly.

Pidgeon gave him a quick backhanded slap. "Big words. Now take your chum and catch a bus home."

Barry rolled on the ground in fetal position, his hands buried between his thighs.

"You've bloody killed me," he croaked.

"No, I haven't," said Pidgeon, walking away. "Enjoy your life of crime, boys. . . ."

Pidgeon felt his racing pulse subside somewhat as he left them. He knew he had looked calm to the two little bastards, but, he told himself, it was a foolish thing for him to have taken them on. These little boys were buying themselves guns these days, and they were just stupid enough to use them. London wasn't New York or Los Angeles yet, but Tony had no doubts about the way the city was heading. A snapshot flashed through his mind: his own body lying on the Queen Anne's Gate cobblestones, shot by a teenager, and the lads at the CID saying, "Tony Pidgeon, he had a great career ahead of him. . . ." Bloody stupid.

And he did have a future on the force. Three years of the Army Police, police training college in record time, a couple of years on the beat, and a decided loathing for criminals added up, in Pidgeon's mind, to the qualifications for the perfect policeman.

Alf Hartley marveled at him. "Our golden boy!" he'd kid. "Our Tony Pidgeon learnt thirty ways to maim a man with a spoon in the army. Just the type of man you want controlling murder in this city." Tony smiled to himself. He liked Alf—a little old-fashioned maybe, but a good bloke. Tony would have his job one day, and that day wasn't too far off. Tony had a weapon that the other charlies didn't have: hate. He hated criminals. Not necessarily because they were bad for society—it was more personal than that. "They think they're better than we are," he'd explain if asked, "and that annoys me."

The autumn sun that shone on the coronation in London couldn't quite break through to shine on a slightly bored, slightly tense Belfast. Coronation Day was a holiday in Ulster as it was elsewhere in the British Isles, but the festivities, restricted to the Protestant sections of town, were watched over closely by British soldiers anxious to avert an incident.

On Kilkenny Street in the Falls Road the patrons of The Lewis stood about drinking and talking while they stared at the cracked black-and-white television set that Denny the barman set up when there was a cup final game or some other major event. It would be a mistake to think that The Lewis patrons were talking bloodthirsty IRA business. Rather, like bar drinkers everywhere, they exchanged jokes and stories, ragged one another, and passed on bits of information about the dog races. Occasionally someone would make a disparaging remark about the scene on television—the coronation. As the state coach passed under Admiralty Arch the BBC camera was able to get a good shot of George VII.

"There he goes," said one man, "the fairy prince...." A ragged line of laughter rippled down the bar. George's fine-featured good looks and unmarried state had called his sexual preferences into doubt, not only in Belfast, but the world over, even in proud, loyal England itself.

Jones, sitting quietly in the corner of the bar, imagined that Aussies in Sydney bars were probably making the same jokes: "Fairy prince," "Virgin Queen," "Queen Georgina." Stupid bastard, thought Jones, why didn't he have the sense to marry? Made the monarchy look bad....

Jones was an Englishman, but he didn't feel uncomfortable in the bar. The lads there—he looked at the six broad backs at the bar—didn't want any trouble, and anyway, Jones knew that he could take care of himself. He was a big man who used his brawn effectively, and he'd been in tougher places than The Lewis: waterfront bars in Aden, places in Kowloon where a man could just disappear, tough bush towns in Uganda and tougher ones in Katanga. Only in Tegucigalpa, Honduras, had

13

he really been worried—he hadn't been able to speak a word of the language, a British accent and a white skin didn't count for a thing, and every damn nig carried a gun. A horrible town in a horrible country. But, he reflected, he had managed to get out of his scrape there without losing too much skin. After that a bar in the Falls Road didn't bother him too much. He took another sip of Special Dark and looked toward the door. His man hadn't shown yet, but he would.

The television camera swung to pick up dignitaries in the parade. For a few seconds it lingered on Hugh Coughlin and his wife, Jennifer—Ambassador and Mrs. Coughlin, the commentator said, representing, along with the Vice-President and the First Lady, the United States of America. The men at the bar cheered for a few seconds.

"Hello, Hughie!" said one. "Dump the Brits and come to Belfast. I'll buy you a pint. . . ."

"And bring the missus," said another.

"Stay home and let the missus come—I'll take care of her!"

Coughlin had recently been appointed to the Court of St. James's, where he had become an instant success on the mainland as well as in Northern Ireland. His father had emigrated from Ulster in the twenties and made himself a fortune in trucking. The feeling in Ireland, north and south, was that Hugh, separated from the old country by only a single generation, would be a good spokesman in America for the six counties. The Kennedys, Jack and Bobby—God rest their souls, the men would say—and Teddy, had lost touch with Ireland; Coughlin hailed from the north, he had the dirt of Ulster under his nails. His wife wasn't Irish but she was tolerated because she was beautiful—"And she wouldn't go marrying some bloody Greek."

The talk at the bar turned to America, a favorite subject. One of the men had been there and retold the same stories about his relatives in South Boston: "Ten thousand quid a year for working on the docks," he said in amazement. "Color TV, washer with spin dryer—the lot!"

"Aye," said another, "but there's trouble in the States, same as anywhere."

14

The men nodded. They drank in silence for a minute.

"God save the King!" came a shout from the doorway. "He'll be buggered by the Coldstreamers tonight. A coronation present from his loyal troops." Leary swayed into the room, unsteadily brushing curly red hair from his forehead. Denny the barman smiled, but the look in his eyes was hostile. The men at the bar shifted uncomfortably. Leary was trouble.

"Drinks for everyone so we can toast our new bloody King," said Leary, dropping a fiver on the bar.

"Just been out thumping a pensioner, have you, Charlie?" asked Billy Hanlon.

Leary looked at Hanlon's considerable form and smiled sweetly. "I'll overlook that, Billy," he said, "on account of the day's glorious occasion."

Leary was a juvenile delinquent who had never grown up, a bullyboy who would steal anything, a braggart with nothing to brag about. He hated most things and most people; more than anything, he wanted to be feared and respected, to be a big shot. Years back he had tried to join the Provos, but even the IRA wouldn't have him—too bloody noisy, can't keep his mouth shut, they said. Leary contented himself with some petty thievery, some breaking and entering, and, when he was in the mood and the odds were with him, a little assault.

From his seat in the shadows Jones observed Leary. He didn't like what he saw. Flynn had chosen Leary as the man they needed but without even speaking a word to him Jones could tell that Leary was unreliable. He would probably not respond well to training, but Jones was a soldier at heart and an order was an order.

Leary's arrival dampened the easy good humor at the bar. One by one the drinkers drained their mugs and said good night to Denny. The barman polished glasses and tried to talk as little as possible to Leary, who drank sullenly at the bar. Abruptly he finished his drink, threw a pound note on the bar (it was his last pound, but even drunk and broke Leary had to impress), and left. Jones gave him a minute and followed him out into the darkening streets.

15

Denny had the bar to himself. He watched the television set a moment longer. "A solemn day, a happy day, a proud day," said the commentator, "proving to the world that whatever her ills, Britain's monarchy endures despite—" Denny switched off the set and returned to his glasses.

CHAPTER TWO

The human body contains about six and a half liters of blood. Most of Brenda Pomeroy's six and a half liters had been drained from her body through a series of incisions stretching from just below her sternum to her pubic bone. There were a number of secondary strikes at her thighs and vulva, none of them serious enough to cause death, although they had bled copiously. Several of her vital organs had been removed and dumped unceremoniously on the floor next to her. All this took place after she died.

Blood from the primary cuts had flowed across the cracked linoleum of her bedroom floor. Some of it congealed in a corner; the remainder, a considerable amount, flowed on, finding its way through the wainscoting, underneath the floorboards and onto the plaster of the ceiling of the room below—the tobacconist's shop, owned by Mr. Austin Ramsay. He noticed the bloodstain, entered Brenda's room to investigate, discovered the body, and called the police. Later editions of the London evening papers would run photographs of Mr. Ramsay pointing at his ceiling. The city editors on the papers were delighted with Miss Pomeroy's demise—people were getting tired of coronation coverage. George had been King for four days.

Tony Pidgeon was sweeping through the revolving doors into Scotland Yard as Alf Hartley was on his way out. They stopped in the lobby, in front of the duty sergeant's desk.

"Evening, Alf," said Pidgeon, "Off home then?"

"That's right, Tony. But you're not." He smiled at the younger man.

Pidgeon looked blankly at Hartley. "I'm not what?"

"You're not going home." Hartley was Pidgeon's immediate superior, a large man, tall but paunchy. His brown hair was going thin on top, "from worrying about the depraved state of mankind," he always said.

"Oh yes I am," said Pidgeon indignantly. "I've been on duty since half-six this morning. I've just finished in court and I'm coming in to tidy up a few things and then I'm off."

"Sorry, Tony, you're on the Pomeroy case."

"The tart?"

"Such language, Tony! Besides, I thought you'd be thanking me."

"A carved-up tart? Not exactly a charming gift."

"But it'll make you a star. The papers love a gruesome prossie-killing. With that million-dollar smile of yours, the press will love you."

"Right. And never leave me alone."

"A little publicity never hurt."

"And I've always fancied going to Hollywood," said Pidgeon. "Well, I'd better get over to what we policemen call 'the scene of the crime.' You don't half keep me busy."

"I'm very impressed with your command of your subject. It's on Frith Street. Over a tobacconist. You can't miss it—it's the one with the bloodstain on the ceiling."

"A clue!" said Pidgeon. "Our man took a stroll across the ceiling after committing the foul deed. Well, I'm off. Cheers, Alf." As he headed for the door he realized that indeed he was elated. The papers could get in the way but they did help your career. The Pomeroy case would be a big one. He could feel it.

"Ah, Tony—" Alf called after him.

18

"Yes, Super?"

"There's just one thing.... Come back here a minute." Hartley creased his red face into a concerned frown and laid a beefy arm on Pidgeon's shoulders. "You're number two on this."

"Who's number one?" asked Pidgeon, puzzled.

"Don't be hard on him," said Alf.

"Don't be hard on who?"

"Smudgie Huddleston. He's heading this one."

"He's what?" Pidgeon couldn't believe his ears. "He hasn't run a show since ... for years. He's been a bleeding typist since I got out of uniform. Besides, he's an *idiot*. That old geezer couldn't find his shoes—"

"Calm yourself, Tony. Smudgie's a good lad. He'll do fine."

"Alf," said Pidgeon through his teeth, "who put him on this? It's a mistake—you know that as well as I do. Get him off. Please." He had raised his voice and it echoed in the lobby. The policeman on duty at the desk stared at him.

"Tony," said Hartley sternly, "this sort of attitude will do you no good. I can't do a bloody thing on this. This comes from the tenth floor. Maybe even from the Gate." The Gate was Yard slang for the Home Office, located in Queen Anne's Gate.

"They can't make divisional assignments."

"No one said life was fair, Tony. Cheer up, lad, you'll still get your name in the papers." Hartley made for the door. "I'd get over there, if I were you. Smudge is already there looking for what you so professionally called 'clues.' " Hartley laughed to himself on his way out of the building. He would chuckle about Pidgeon's discomfort all the way home to Camberwell.

"Old bastard," said Pidgeon after him.

Although he wasn't as young as he used to be, Smudge Huddleston found himself taking the stairs two at a time to Brenda Pomeroy's former residence. He was sure that he'd get moved off this case before it got anywhere, but he wanted to get something done before the ax fell. He was determined to

19

show his superiors and the youngsters in the CID that there was life in Huddleston yet.

A constable stood in front of the door on the second floor. He was a young man with a beard.

"Here for a look round, Inspector?"

"That's right," said Smudge.

"It'll be gruesome," said the young man solicitously.

Smudge looked at him, annoyed. "I'm on this case, Constable, I'm not a bloody tourist."

"Sorry, sir."

Smudge opened the door to the bedroom. The body and the photographers had gone and the fingerprint lads were going over every inch of the room. Davey Forbes, a fingerprint officer, watched his squad critically through bottle-thick spectacles. There were hundreds, maybe thousands of prints in the room. There would be, he reasoned, in a tart's bedroom.

"Hello, Davey," said Huddleston. "Anything interesting?" He dug in his overcoat pocket for his pipe and pouch.

Forbes had left Glasgow twenty years before but the burr hung in his voice still. "Hello, Smudgie. It seems that Miss Pomeroy did a great deal of entertaining."

Smudge nodded. "Found a weapon?"

"Nothing." Forbes pulled his glasses from his nose and polished them meditatively with the end of his tie. "You on this one, Smudge?"

"That's right," said Huddleston. "Why does that surprise everyone so much?" He chewed on the mouthpiece of his pipe.

Davey Forbes shifted his weight a bit. "Looks a bit like South America, that one, doesn't it?"

"What does?" asked Smudge, puzzled.

"That bloodstain. See, here's Brazil. That bit sticking down is Argentina. . . ."

"You're not a well man, Davey."

"Just highly imaginative."

"Where's the body?" Smudge lit his pipe.

"On the way to the morgue. She's a mess. About twenty different pieces. Either someone took a very great exception to Miss Pomeroy or we've got another Jack the Ripper."

"It's a possibility, Davey."

"Your problem, Smudge."

Huddleston stared at the grimy window and considered Forbes's statement. "Do we know anything about her?"

"Not much. The usual. Young. She has a Nottingham address on her license. She's probably got a pimp someplace."

"The bloke downstairs, the landlord . . ."

"His name is Ramsay. I think he gave us a statement," said Davey.

"I don't suppose he heard anything? Saw anyone?"

"He isn't here at night. He lives in Putney."

Smudge nodded as if he expected Mr. Ramsay to live in Putney. "Any idea how long she's been dead?"

"An educated guess, about three days. The Med Squad will let you know."

Smudge nodded to himself again. "Probably her pimp. Have they gone through her handbag?"

"Compact, five quid, lipstick, the usual," said a detective sergeant standing behind them. "And this . . ." He held up a photograph.

Davey Forbes looked at it first. He whistled. "No, I don't think you should look at this, Smudge. Not without a note from your missus." He handed Smudge the picture.

It was a Polaroid that showed two women naked, save for what Soho theatrical costumers would consider tribal dress, a cross between Hawaiian dancing girl and Zulu warrior. The two women were entwined, not quite intimately enough to bring down the wrath of the Vice Squad. The picture had been snapped on a stage; over the proscenium, picked out in glitter, was the name Club Eroticus.

"This is our lassie," said Forbes, pointing to one of the women. "The one on the bottom. She looks very young." He sighed and then added, "Club Eroticus, it's a hole."

"How do you know?" said Smudge, looking away from the photograph, which embarrassed him a little, and staring at the bloodstain instead, trying to see Brazil.

"I took a bunch of print men from the Tokyo force there. They were here on a fact-finding mission. They loved it."

21

"You dirty old man," said Tony Pidgeon, coming into the room.

"Well, tough Tony Pidgeon. Come to put bamboo slivers up our bums?"

"I might. . . . Hello, Smudge. We're together on this one."

"I heard," said Smudge, his chin resting on his chest.

Crikey, said Forbes to himself, what a pair.

"I'm sure we'll get on together," said Huddleston.

"Hope so," said Pidgeon, a trifle surly.

I doubt it, thought Forbes. In all his years on the force he had never seen a more mismatched pair. Huddleston hadn't been on a big case in ages. A bit of legwork for the other lads, some background information maybe. But mostly it was typing reports and fetching cups of tea in some anonymous office in the Yard. It wasn't that he was a bad policeman, but he'd somehow never amounted to much. Most of the blokes figured that he was just putting in his time and the Yard was content to let him go quietly. Huddleston was past it, it was that simple. Pidgeon was a different sort altogether. He'd break your bloody arm for a lead. Smart, quick, and a bit too anxious to get ahead in the department. Forbes hoped that Smudgie knew he was in for a bumpy ride.

A photographer methodically made his way around the room photographing the murder scene from all angles. The sharp flash split the room every few seconds.

"Well," said Forbes, "I'm off; my lads here can manage without me. We'll run the lifts tomorrow if we get them all tonight. I wouldn't hope for too much. . . ."

"How many are there?" asked Pidgeon.

"We have enough prints in this room to populate a good-sized town," said Forbes cheerily. "About the size of Cardiff, I should say. Cheers, lads."

"Bye, Davey," said Huddleston. He lowered himself into the room's only armchair, the plastic cover squeaking under him. He rubbed his temples and watched the Fingerprint Squad slowly work their way round the room. "I'm exhausted," said Smudge quietly.

Pidgeon looked at the ceiling. Granddad duty, he thought.

22

"Well," said Smudge, "got any ideas?"

"Well, they found only five quid in her purse. . . ."

"Doubt if it was robbery," said Smudge meditatively.

Pidgeon managed to repress his impatience. "I'm not saying it was. She didn't have much money and she couldn't go home to her ponce without a good score, so I reckon one of two things happened. She offered to do some rough stuff for more than her usual fee and ended up getting a little more than she bargained for. Or she tried to nick some money from her punter and he turned nasty."

Huddleston appeared not to have heard. He stared at the photograph of some American heartthrob over her bed. "Who can say?"

Pidgeon sighed. It was going to be a long case.

"Tell me, Tony—I can call you Tony?"

"That's my name," said Pidgeon, watching one of the print men dust the bedside table.

"Tony," Huddleston started again, "if you were a tart bringing a punter home on a cold night, what's the first thing you'd ask him?"

The question embarrassed Pidgeon. Huddleston sounded like an Agatha Christie character.

"I would ask him," said Pidgeon nastily, "if he intended to stay long. . . . I don't know. What are you on about?"

"I'll tell you what you'd ask him. You would want fifty p for the meter."

"So?" Pidgeon asked irritably.

"I'll bet you that the coin is in there with our man's prints."

One of the Print Squad, a fellow on his knees dusting the wainscoting, looked up. "Sorry, Inspector. We emptied the box. There's not a single readable print in the lot."

"Just an idea," said Smudge.

Tony Pidgeon lived in a part of London that its residents thought of as "smart" Chelsea but that was probably part of "up-and-coming" Pimlico. Either way, he couldn't afford his modest two-room flat. He could have moved farther out of the city, to Hanwell or Hammersmith, but he felt somehow that he was too young to be so far away from the center of things. That he did very little besides work and sleep had frequently occurred to him; he might as well have lived in Chichester, for all the good it did him living in the center of London. But he wouldn't give it up, despite the hole it made in his pay; he tolerated the deafening bus traffic on Lower Sloane Street and reasoned that what he spent in rent he saved in transport.

He closed the door of his flat and flung himself down on the couch in the tiny living room. He was tired, but before his closed eyes flashed the mustachioed, complacent, pipe-smoking face of Smudge Huddleston. Although Pidgeon was glad to be on the Pomeroy case, he half hoped that some bloodstained blubbering pimp was at that moment turning himself in at West Central, saying, "I done it."

He opened his eyes. Hanging over the bricked-up fireplace was an original work of art. He hated it. It was a few square feet of plastic sheeting, erupting at irregular intervals with pustules of luridly painted fiberglass. He had slept with its creator a few times, a well-intentioned girl he'd met at The Antelope, not really his type. Before embarking on an artistic career she'd spent her life in tartan skirts or jodhpurs in some chocolate-box village in Hampshire, where her father, by virtue of being extremely rich, was the local magistrate. She still referred to him as Daddy, as in, "Daddy is a philistine, but a poppet nonetheless." The philistine/poppet paid for her artistic Chelsea flat and had probably paid for the expensive frame job on Pidgeon's painting. She had painted it in honor of Pidgeon's profession, titling it *London Underworld*.

Dinner loomed before him. Pidgeon had caught the cooking disease the year before from a French girl he wanted to impress, who had au-paired for the large flat that took up the top two floors of his building. He had resolutely tried to teach himself the finer points of haute cuisine ever since, although she had long ago returned to Rouen, having slept with him only once. He couldn't really remember how the sex was (he had been drunk) but he knew, without a doubt, that his cooking was horrible. His *blanquette de veau* came out tough and blah, the *coq*

24

au vin looked as villainous as it would at a fine French restaurant but tasted—there was no other way to describe it—the way burnt paint smells, and his one attempt at a soufflé (soufflé au fromage et asperges) had resulted in his having to throw out a dish that had cost him £4 at the Reject Pottery Shop. More often than not, late evenings would find him at The Antelope with burnt hands and foul humor, eating a meat pie and wondering why he bothered.

Luckily, tonight he didn't have to worry about failing again—he didn't have time. Smudge Huddleston had insisted that they investigate Pomeroy's connection with Club Eroticus. They had gone round to the club earlier but it had been locked up tight. Smudge had decided that they would have to check it out that night.

"Time and tide wait for no man," Huddleston had reminded him.

"Bugger you," said Pidgeon to *London's Underworld.* He wondered if Huddleston had arranged this evening out so he could examine the "100's of International Beauties" advertised in Club Eroticus's dingy marquee.

Abruptly he swung off the couch and looked at his watch. Seven o'clock. There were three hours before he had to meet Granddad. He walked into his bedroom and began to take off his clothes. He could do with a shower. He looked at the telephone next to his large brass bed (another waste of money, he told himself) and wondered when it had rung last.

Smudge Huddleston lived in exactly the sort of place Pidgeon was anxious to avoid, in Mortlake. He owned his own home, did a bit of do-it-yourself on weekends, and was an expert on the history and geography of his own little corner of London. Mortlake, he would tell regulars at The Spurs, was steeped in history. If someone asked what, for instance, Smudge would trot out his trump card. The famous explorer Sir Richard Burton, who had almost discovered the source of the White Nile (but didn't, someone at the bar would say), was buried in the cemetery of the Catholic church by the railway track. His tombstone was shaped like an Arab tent. "Very picturesque," Smudge would assure them.

Huddleston's house had a tiny front garden in which he would place a deck chair when it was fine and in which his wife, Irene, had tried to plant roses. They did not prosper. But that didn't bother Smudge. As he turned the corner into Dominion Crescent (all of the streets in the neighborhood had suitably imperial names: Star of India Terrace, Ashanti Gardens, Omdurman Close) and caught sight of the house he had lived in for almost thirty years—a house indistinguishable from the one on its left and right—he was as proud as a country squire surveying his family seat.

On his way into the house he met his twenty-year-old son, Rodney, on his way out.

"Evening, son," said Smudge.

"Screw you, copper," said Rodney, pushing past him.

The faintest look of hurt framed Smudge's eyes. He had long since stopped trying to understand his son.

"Rodney!" shouted Irene from the kitchen. "Don't talk to your father like that."

"Going out, son?" said Smudge to the closing front door.

Irene entered the cramped hallway. "I'm sorry, Sammy," she said. "I don't know why he acts that way."

"Leave the lad, Irene. He'll grow out of it."

She kissed Huddleston affectionately on the forehead. "He doesn't deserve a father like you. . . . How was your day?"

Smudge went into the front room and lowered himself into his armchair. "Things are looking up," he said.

"How's that, dear?"

"I'm running an investigation," he said, a touch of pride in his voice. Apart from his superiors, there was only one person in the world he wanted to impress: Irene. Sometimes during the long train rides home he'd remember the day they met during the war, and their courtship—him in the artillery, Irene in Queen Alexandra's Imperial Military Nursing Corps. The happiest days of his life. When he looked at Irene he never saw the stout woman with a slightly harried look that she had become; the loose skin around her neck, the black hair streaked with gray, the worried look in her brown eyes were the same component parts of the slim, vivacious girl he met at the NAAFI the day Mountbatten took over command of the Far East. He loved her then, he loved her now. Sometimes late at night he'd whisper in her ear, without embarrassment: "Pretty as a summer morning is my Irene."

Irene showed genuine pleasure at his news. "Sammy, that's wonderful. I always said they didn't use you enough." Her face clenched for a minute. "Nothing dangerous?"

"No, love, nothing dangerous. I'll be going out tonight though—part of the case."

"Yes, dear," she said. "Have a cup of tea." She never asked him questions.

From the shed in their back garden came the sudden and deafening sound of the rock band of which Rodney was the lead guitarist. They were called The Runs and they were working on a new song, written by Rodney, called "Living in a Padded Cell." Pain creased Huddleston's face as the sound forced its way into the room.

"Shall I go and tell them to keep it down?" asked Irene nervously. She didn't like facing The Runs when they were assembled.

"No," said Huddleston above the din, "don't bother."

"Whatever shall we do with him?" asked Irene plaintively.

"It's a stage he's going through, love. He'll come round. Don't worry...."

Irene thought it was more likely that Rodney would murder them both, but didn't say so.

CHAPTER THREE

Club Eroticus looked much like the other half dozen tawdry flesh traps that lined Frith Street. At street level it was just another brightly lit doorway leading to a set of dubious-looking stairs descending to basement level. Around the doorway were some photographs in cracked plastic frames of the club's featured performers. Women showing their breasts pouted and leered from the photos, trying to live up to their outlandish stage names, which seemed to follow a pattern of an appropriately feminine first name coupled with a surname taken from some major natural disaster—Tamara Volcano, Melissa Typhoon; one had enterprisingly named herself Tiffany Krakatoa—meant to connote uncontrollable passion. In Tony Pidgeon they raised only embarrassment, and they seemed to affect Huddleston not at all.

Huddleston led the way in. A young man in a pin-striped suit sat reading a newspaper just inside the door, behind a tiny desk. He looked up from his paper and said without much enthusiasm: "Welcome, gents. Best show in London." He had heavy-lidded, bored eyes.

"How much?" asked Pidgeon.

"Six quid apiece," said the young man, thinking to himself that the older of the two customers looked suspiciously like a copper.

"Two," said Huddleston, "and two receipts."

"What?" said the doorkeeper.

"A receipt. I want two receipts."

The young man shrugged and wrote on a piece of paper. He handed it to Pidgeon.

"To get reimbursed," said Huddleston.

"Why not just tell them we're Old Bill, Smudge?" said Pidgeon as they made their way downstairs.

A man in a tuxedo who had once described himself in criminal court as "the maître d' in a West End restaurant" met them at the base of the stairs.

"Follow me please, gents." He led them into a smoky room in which a number of men sat at tables ranged around a low stage, the stage in the photograph of Brenda Pomeroy. The men hunched over their drinks, their eyes flicking nervously over Pidgeon and Huddleston. They would not relax until the show began, giving them a focus for their guilty glances.

Disco music, played at just under earsplitting volume, pumped into the room from cracked speakers behind the stage.

"Bloody noisy," said Smudge.

Pidgeon just nodded and wished he were at home.

"Fancy a drink, gents?" asked the maître d' in a tone of voice that suggested that if they didn't they would be distinctly unwelcome.

"A brandy," said Pidgeon, knowing that what he'd get would be coarse enough to run a lawnmower.

"Just a lager for me," said Huddleston.

As their eyes became accustomed to the light, each man knew that they should talk to each other. Piegeon knew, however, that apart from a curse or two he had nothing to say. Luckily a waiter returned with their drinks and delayed the need for conversation. He placed the drinks on the table without a word and Pidgeon seized his, more to have something to do than from thirst, and sipped. The brandy immediately en-

29

gaged in combat with the omelette (which had become scrambled eggs with mushrooms once he started cooking) that he had eaten for dinner.

"Been in a place like this before?" asked Huddleston.

"In the army," said Pidgeon.

"There was a war on when I was in the army," said Huddleston, shifting.

Abruptly the show began. The first girl, Angelica Earthquake, was surprisingly pretty. She wore a matching set of sequined shorts and top, together the size of a table napkin, which she shucked immediately to stand completely naked in front of the crowd. Pidgeon heard Huddleston draw strongly on his pipe.

Angelica picked up a microphone and lip-synched a verse or two of the song belting out behind her. Pidgeon stared at her face. It was fresh and open, and she seemed amazingly at ease starkers in front of a bunch of drunken men. She didn't seem to be enjoying herself much, though; she had the same slightly bored, slightly resentful expression that he saw on the faces of check-out girls in supermarkets. In a curious way that reassured him. He hated the fake "fuck me" coarseness of the strippers he and his comrades-in-arms had stared at drunkenly on the Reeperbahn.

The lighting switched to a dizzying strobe, catching Angelica in a series of jerky stilted movements. As she passed the microphone down between her legs, the sound track blared the breathy moans of a prerecorded orgasm, presumably Angelica's.

Act followed act, all much the same. The performers all carried some kind of phallic prop that they placed in their mouths, on their breasts, and when the lighting got dim, between their legs; there it was hard to tell exactly what they did with them. Desultory clapping followed each act. Casting his mind back over the hour or so of pink flesh he had watched, except for Angelica and a black girl who had sprung out of a papier-mâché clamshell, Pidgeon could remember very little of the gyrating, goosebumped flesh he had seen. He had had enough. The girl in Brenda Pomeroy's photograph hadn't shown up.

"She's not here," said Pidgeon. "The turnover rate in a place like this must be enormous."

Huddleston nodded. "Let's go have a word with the management." He signaled the waiter. "Where's the manager?"

The waiter surveyed them coldly. "There's a problem?"

"No," said Pidgeon, "we just want a word with your boss." He stared at the waiter. He knew he looked and sounded menacing. The thought pleased him a bit.

"He's not here."

"I have a feeling he is," said Pidgeon, taking out his police identity card.

"Through the door behind the bar. The one marked Private," he said, smiling weakly.

Smudge led the way. Sitting at a table, reading the *Evening Standard*, was a man in a suit. His hair was neatly combed. He knew instantly who Smudge was.

"She never stuck it in!" he shouted, leaping to his feet.

"What?" said Huddleston blankly.

"She only looked like she did. It's the lighting. Honest."

"What?" asked Smudge again.

"Sit down," said Pidgeon to the man. "He thinks we're here to talk to him about presenting a lewd and indecent public spectacle," he explained to Huddleston. "It's none of our business, chum, so relax."

But the man didn't relax. His eyes narrowed. "What do you want?"

"What's your name?" asked Pidgeon.

"Larry."

"Larry," said Pidgeon pleasantly. "Larry what?"

"Larry Hill."

"All right, Mr. Hill," said Pidgeon. "I am Detective Sergeant Pidgeon and this is Detective Inspector Huddleston. We would like to know if you recognize either of these women." He slid the photograph forward on the table.

Hill scarcely looked at it. "No."

Pidgeon lit a cigarette. He rarely smoked but it made an effective prop. He exhaled. "Come on now, Mr. Hill, you see the name over the stage. Think."

31

"I see a lot of naked birds."

"How would you like Club Eroticus to be visited six times a night, seven days a week, by the members of London's fine Vice Squad? You know the Vice boys, don't you, Mr. Hill? They're the ones that don't pay six quid to get in. Permanent members of the Club Eroticus, you might say. Things are very quiet at Vice just now. I'm sure that my friends there would be glad to help me out. . . . Should I go on, Mr. Hill?"

"The bird on top is named Meg. She's left London. . . ."

"Where'd she go?" asked Smudge.

"Up north. Leeds, I think."

"And the other one?"

"She used to come in here every so often. Not a regular. She'd get a customer to order champagne and the club would split fifty-fifty with her."

"Her name?"

"She had a dozen. Marilyn was one, Linda, Brenda, changed every night. . . ." Hill squinted at the photograph. "Here. That's the tart that got done, isn't it?" He looked at the front page of his newspaper. "That's her, isn't it?" He looked genuinely scared.

"You're not as stupid as you look, Mr. Hill," said Pidgeon pleasantly.

"Listen," said Hill feverishly, "I'm not mixed up in anything like that. She'd come in once in a while, fill in an act if a girl was out. That's all. I don't know who'd do her. Honest."

"She got a ponce?" asked Huddleston.

"I dunno."

"Come on, Mr. Hill," said Pidgeon.

"Really, I dunno. She was paid direct. I never dealt with her man."

"She been in here recently?"

"I haven't seen her in ages. That's the gospel."

Huddleston and Pidgeon exchanged glances.

"Honest," repeated Hill.

Pidgeon headed for the door. "We'll be in touch, Mr. Hill." On the street he said, "Greasy little bastard."

32

"Not very savory," agreed Huddleston. "Not very helpful, either."

"I think we better go see Colin the Leb."

"Who?"

The streets had grown empty. Only the men running the few late-night joints and the men who patronized them were on the streets. The last late buses roared along Shaftesbury Avenue.

"Colin the Leb is a friend of mine," said Pidgeon, "and he owes me a favor."

Colin the Leb's office was an open-sided phone box set on the pavement in front of an amusement arcade in Dean Street, from which he took orders for small amounts of drugs delivered at any time of the day or night to any part of central London. "I never close" was his motto, and Colin did his best to live up to it by hardly ever sleeping. Rumor had it that Colin's business had earned him enough to buy a very nice little place in Ladbroke Grove, but if that was true he was rarely in residence. Every few months he'd disappear for a few weeks, returning fit and tanned and eager to get back to work. He loved his job.

When on duty he took staggering amounts of Dexedrine and was rather thin as a result. The healthy tan of his last Mediterranean trip had long since left him and his Lebanese coloring was now rather chalky. He wore a denim suit over a Jermyn Street shirt; both garments hung on him like limp sails. He was staring intently at the screen of a Space Invaders video game, the one closest to the front door, knocking off the enemy forces with ease. The game beeped and squealed in microchipped annoyance.

"Evening, Colin," said Pidgeon, clapping him on the shoulder.

"Fuck off, Tony," said Colin, without looking up from the screen. "I haven't done anything."

"Know Brenda Pomeroy?"

"Who?" said Colin, his eyes riveted to the spaceships careening across the screen.

"Another one with a poor memory," said Pidgeon to

33

Smudge. "Shall I go tear the phone out of the box?"

"Come on, Tony," Colin whined, "you know I don't go in for tarts."

"Listen, Colin, you're awake twenty-four hours a day. Did you see her a couple of nights ago?"

"No." Colin shot down a death star and scored a hundred points.

Smudge felt a bit out of his element. It had been years since he worked the street, and things had changed. Pidgeon handled these people well.

"Colin," said Pidgeon reproachfully, "we've been friends a long time."

"I don't know anything."

The phone rang and Pidgeon planted his hand squarely on Colin's chest, holding him effortlessly at arm's length. Pidgeon picked up the receiver, sure that whoever was at the other end was in no condition to distinguish between Colin's voice and his own. Colin swore silently and reached ineffectually for the phone. The other patrons of the arcade watched nervously.

"Tony, give me that bleedin' phone."

"Yeah," said Pidgeon into the phone.

"Tony, please."

"Yeah," said Pidgeon again, trying to make out the order of the very stoned person on the other end of the line.

"Where?" he asked. "Hang on." Pidgeon turned to Colin. "What are you charging for a gram of coke these days, Colin? Or should I just tell him you've been arrested? Or are you going to help us a bit?"

"Gimme that phone." Colin snatched it from Pidgeon's hand. "Listen," he said, "I'll call you back." He hung up. "Christ, what a rotten thing to do. . . ."

"I didn't tell him you'd been run in," said Pidgeon innocently.

"Could've bloody ruined me."

"I'm tired of playing, Colin," said Pidgeon. "Tell us what we want to know and we'll be on our way."

"I haven't seen her," said Colin sullenly, "but I know she's got a ponce named Mac."

"Not much of a name."

"Mac's not much of a fella."

"Where is he?"

"How should I know?"

"Tony is getting angry with Colin," said Pidgeon.

"Try the New Yorker Club."

"Thanks, Colin, you're a pal. . . . Come on, Smudgie."

Huddleston followed Pidgeon out onto the street; he felt a bit useless.

The New Yorker Club was almost identical to Club Eroticus: seedy, smoky, dark, and noisy. Huddleston and Pidgeon didn't bother watching the show this time; they just showed their cards to a waiter and he, anxious to preserve his probation, obligingly pointed out Mac.

He sat at a table at the back of the room, drinking deep from a glass of gin and bitters. He scarcely looked up when the two policemen sat down, one on each side of him.

"Knew you'd get here eventually," he said. Pidgeon and Huddleston tensed. It was the opening line of so many confessions. For a second Pidgeon began to look forward to bragging the next day about cracking this case in a single night.

"What's that mean?" he asked.

"I knew you'd show up to ask me about Brenda."

Huddleston looked at Mac curiously. He was thickset, a few pounds shy of being fat. He looked like a thousand other men who made their living on the fringes of crime: red-faced from drinking too much, choleric from staying up late doing it, and tense from being scared most of the time. Huddleston noted with surprise that Mac looked as if he had been crying.

"I didn't kill 'er," said Mac.

"Are we supposed to take your word for that?" asked Huddleston.

"I don't expect you to understand," said Mac to the table, "but I loved that girl."

"Right," said Pidgeon unpleasantly, "every time she opened her legs."

"It wasn't like that," Mac whined.

35

"When did you see her last?"

"Wednesday. Four days ago." Mac stared into his drink.

"Alone?"

"What?"

"Alone. Was she alone when you saw her?"

"Oh—yeah."

"Any ideas who might have wanted to do this to her?" asked Huddleston.

"No. Everybody liked 'er . . . really."

"Spare us," said Pidgeon.

He took another swallow from his drink. "The newspapers said 'the mangled remains.' Have you seen 'er? Is it 'orrible?"

"She looks like a rhubarb pie," said Pidgeon, "and you've only got yourself to blame, Mac, my lad."

" 'ow do you mean?" said Mac hotly. "I took 'er in. Looked after 'er. I introduced 'er to my friends."

"And one of them sliced her open."

Mac looked as if he had been slapped. His lower lip trembled.

"She have any regular customers?"said Smudge gently. He couldn't help feeling sorry for this man.

Mac shook his head. "She hadn't been working long."

"Anyone front for her? A cabby? Newsagent?" demanded Pidgeon. Most London prostitutes were contacted through off-duty cab drivers cruising Soho, or via discreet signs placed in newsstand windows. (SANDRA, FRENCH MASSAGE, CALL . . .).

"She wasn't bringing in enough to justify the expense," he said, as if he were the chairman of BP.

"So there was no one to filter out the psychos on the street," said Pidgeon. "As I said, Mac, blame yourself. . . . Anything else, Smudge?"

Smudge shook his head."No, nothing else."

"Let's clear off, then."

As they left, Mac drained his glass. "I 'ope you find the bastard," he called after them, "really I do. . . ."

"Pathetic," said Pidgeon.

———

About the time Huddleston and Pidgeon were leaving the New Yorker Club, the King of England was lighting a cigar in his private sitting room in Buckingham Palace's north wing. It had been an extremely long day, filled with Royal dispatch boxes and hundreds of people whose smiling courteous faces George could hardly remember.

Every morning he received the first of a series of government briefing papers, ranging in subject from Scottish forestry to finance. He read them all, though in many cases he was definitely out of his depth. He'd have to ask Astley to schedule further briefings on the economic issues: numbers had never been his strong point.

The room he sat in was, by palace standards, a modest one. It contained a few paintings—an excellent Rubens over the fireplace, a Turner seascape over the leather couch on which he sat. A color television set stood on top of a low bookcase running along one wall. The bookcase also held stereo equipment and some records.

George was a handsome young man, with blond hair falling forward onto his forehead, in what *Harper's & Queen* magazine called "a charming offhand manner." His bearing, although regal when it had to be, could be described in much the same way. In the year between George's assuming the throne and the actual coronation, word had gone out that ceremony was to be kept at a minimum, a change that pleased the younger staff but displeased some of their elders. "A king should act like a king," said Walter Higgins, who had polished Royal silver for forty years in the strong room deep in the cellars below the kitchen. "He has a position to maintain."

George drew on his cigar and thought about what he had read that day. He was, despite what some Labor back-benchers might have thought, no fool and it was clear to him that behind the calm, properly modulated tone employed by the writers of the Royal briefings, Britain's problems, the dry, hard rock of Europe's decline, were considerable. A précis of a report from some BP engineers announced that North Sea oil fields were now on the brink of depletion; the minutes of a secret meeting of economic ministers of the EEC in Brussels showed that the market was getting a bit fed up with their British members: despite lowered requirements, Britain's bills still weren't being paid on time.

A communiqué from NATO suggested that Britain might up her forces on the Rhine, with a note from the Minister of Defense pointing out that the money wasn't there to do it. A Ministry of Employment "action study" reported that there was serious discontent among the miners and suggested that the Welsh pits might be closed by labor disputes as the winter wore on. The Governor of the Bank of England, in a note to the Chancellor of the Exchequer, suggested that Britain's strong pound ($3.20 at the close) was ruinously high. Perhaps time was right for a fourteen percent devaluation. George took another pull on his cigar. It was, in a word, grim.

There was a knock at the door, and Geoffrey Stanhope, George's equerry, looked in.

"Done your homework?" he asked, smiling.

"Geoffrey," said George, "come in. Have a drink."

Geoffrey Stanhope was, as the papers pointed out, a figure from another age. He was tall and fair, officer and gentleman, "the kind of man I'm told didn't come back from Flanders," observed his commanding officer in the Guards.

Geoffrey poured two fingers of brandy in a glass and waved the decanter at George. "You?"

"No, I've got some, thank you."

Stanhope settled in an armchair facing George. "Busy day?"

"Horrible."

"Things should settle down when the coronation fever has died. You're a national plaything at the moment."

"Wonderful," said George. "What's on for tomorrow?"

"Commonwealth Development Corporation for lunch, a gala festival celebrating the Tricentenary of the Royal Society of Civil Engineers in the evening. I think you've got the P.M. in the afternoon."

"Charming," said George.

"You'll love it," said Stanhope.

"I'm afraid I don't know much about civil engineering. Not my strong suit."

"You could talk to them about aircraft. That might mean something to them."

"I hope so."

"Besides, you can always get Astley to brief you tomorrow." Sir Randolph Astley was the King's private secretary.

"Astley knows everything," said George with a smile.

"Not really," said Stanhope, "but he'll teach you to be an accomplished liar."

It was unusual for equerries to talk so loosely with the monarchs they served, although the job was supposed to include aspects of a live-in companion. Stanhope and George had known each other for years. Indeed, as far as it was possible to grow up with the heir to the throne, Stanhope had done it. He had been a monitor in George's dormitory at school, had crammed him in Moderns at Oxford. They had been friends for years, scrapping and squabbling as children, dreaming and bragging as youths; it was in each other's company that they had both gotten drunk for the first time, on the floor of the butler's pantry of the Stanhope country place in Wiltshire. George had been sixteen, Geoffrey a year older. Later they had parted company long enough for them to serve in the armed forces, George in the navy and Stanhope in the army, but they had never lost touch.

"I've just been looking over some information sent to me this afternoon."

"Pretty dull stuff, I should imagine," said Stanhope.

"Pretty frightening, actually."

"How so?"

"We're just about bankrupt." George sipped his drink.

"We've been just about bankrupt for years," said Stanhope.

"It's rather distressing," said George earnestly. "And I'm not just saying that. Monsieur Franval wants us to pull out of the Common Market. That would be damn embarrassing."

"Said that in Brussels?" asked Stanhope.

"I thought that meeting was secret."

"One hears things," said Stanhope airily. "Can't keep a secret in this place."

"Yes, he said it in Brussels yesterday afternoon."

"Those frogs," said Stanhope in a false basso.

"You don't seem very concerned, Geoffrey," said George, a little annoyed.

"I am, really. But I'm afraid that the British malaise is just about incurable. And there's very little that can be done about it. It's a terrible thing to realize, but there you are."

"Nothing for the national plaything to do but have his face put on stamps," said George ruefully.

"They'd be worthless without your face on them," said Stanhope with a smile. He had been warned that the properly controlled atmosphere of palace life might have this sort of effect on a young man who carried all the accoutrements of power but not power itself. He could sympathize with George, whose job demanded evenhandedness, almost blandness, in all things.

"I'm sure there's something I could do."

"Steady, I doubt it. You've got a left wing ready to bite your head off. You know the kind of groaning there was over the civil list last year." The civil list was the amount of money paid by Parliament for the upkeep of the Royal Family; it ran to several million pounds annually. "And don't forget you've got the Imperial Loonies and the other right-wing groups that would love a chance to have a go at the left." The Imperial Loonies was Stanhope's pet name for the Imperial Brotherhood, a political faction with no representation but growing support, which advocated the reestablishment of a British Empire. The Imperial Brotherhood had already fought a number of bloody, pitched battles with the Socialist Workers Party.

"You make it sound like we're on the verge of civil war, Geoffrey."

"No, not really. Not in England," said Stanhope, finishing his drink. "I'm going to bed. Good night, George."

"Good night, Geoffrey."

Stanhope left and George listened to his footsteps recede down the Long Gallery. He drew on his cigar, but found it had gone out and dropped it in the ashtray. He got up, stretched, and walked to the desk that stood in front of a tall window overlooking the vast Palace Gardens that stretched away, spot-lit at intervals, toward Belgravia.

Abruptly he picked up the telephone. The light on the panel next to the number lit and George imagined the light going on next to his number in the communications room several floors below him. A Blues corporal was probably all ready to write it down in his log: Extension One, 1:13 a.m. . . . George held the receiver in his hand and then replaced it.

Why bother? he asked himself, and went to bed.

Stanhope settled in his room not far down the gallery and, not for the first time, reflected on how naïve George was. It distressed him and he wondered if there wasn't some way to temper it, to pull his head from the clouds.

Stanhope sat on the edge of his bed and slipped off his shoes. He wondered whose duty it was to tell George that he must tread as quiet and as soft a path as possible. Stanhope let his body go limp and felt his shoulders sag. He hoped it wasn't his duty to say anything.

A few moments later, as he brushed his teeth, he said aloud, his words obstructed by the toothbrush: "Why the hell doesn't he get married?"

CHAPTER FOUR

Readers of London's morning papers, scanning the headlines over a second cup of tea or on the train to work, were treated to varying descriptions of the murder of Brenda Pomeroy. The unabashedly sensational press, the *Sun,* the *Daily Mirror,* and others, gave the story banner headlines on their front pages. JACK'S BACK! proclaimed the *Sun* in twelvepoint: "The shadows of a Victorian nightmare stalk the sinful streets of Soho...." Readers skipping down the column were informed that "Brenda Pomeroy, 17, described by police as a 'known prostitute', was found in her place of business by her landlord, Mr. Austin Ramsay, a tobacconist. 'It was horrible,' Mr. Ramsay told the *Sun* last night, 'All chopped up, she was....'"

Under the headline ONCE MORE WITH FEELING, the *Daily Mirror* carried the same quote from Mr. Ramsay, but scooped the *Sun:* "The Mirror has learned that two crack detectives from Scotland Yard, Inspector Samuel Huddleston and his longtime partner, Detective Tony Pidgeon, have been assigned to the case." The *Mirror* went on to quote a source at Scotland Yard (in whose remarks insiders could see the hand of Alf Hartley) as saying "They're the best. They personify all that is admirable in the British policeman." The *Mirror* closed its story by promising to let its readers know the minute Jack struck again.

The slightly more restrained *Daily Express,* under the headline BIZARRE SLAYING OF WEST END GOODTIME GIRL, suggested that London's streets, once the safest in the world, were becoming "as bloodstained as the dark thoroughfares of New York and Los Angeles." The *Express,* too, quoted a source in Scotland Yard as saying, "If anyone can crack this case, it's them [Huddleston, Pidgeon]. They're professionals to the backbone." The *Express* had also managed to get hold of a photograph of Pidgeon which they ran over the caption "Detective Pidgeon, professional."

The Times and the *Telegraph* covered the story on their inner pages. *The Times* (WEST END MURDER) recapped the stories of both the original Jack the Ripper of 1888 and the Yorkshire Ripper of the 1970s. It also pointed out that while the first Ripper had never been caught, the Yorkshire Ripper had been apprehended after a five-year investigation.

The *Telegraph* carried the story in a similar mode, adding that the police "while not wishing to excite panic advised women in the Greater London area to exercise caution when travelling late at night."

Of the five papers only *The Times* and the *Telegraph* carried another story quite unrelated to the Pomeroy murder. AMBASSADOR COUGHLIN TO VISIT ULSTER: "The American Ambassador leaves London this afternoon for a twenty-four-hour tour of Northern Ireland. . . ." The *Telegraph* noted that "Ambassador Coughlin, a popular figure among the Catholic minority in Northern Ireland, will not be accompanied by Mrs. Coughlin. . . ."

Headaches, thought Jack Sweeney, this job is nothing but headaches. He never thought he'd miss Washington, scrabbling up and down the corridors of the Rayburn Building, but here in England he found himself missing *Albany,* for Christ sake, where he had started working for Coughlin during his first term as governor.

Sweeney was sitting in the officer's club lounge of Lakenheath Air Force Base, and although it was only eight o'clock in the morning and the officer's bar was officially closed, he was nursing a cold, cold, cold Budweiser. Lakenheath is an American base and Sweeney, Ambassador Coughlin's right-hand man, "Hughie's fixer," was taking the opportunity to have a nice cold American beer instead of the lukewarm British junk he could never get used to.

Overhead, an American F15 roared low over the camp, followed twenty-five seconds later by another. Routine morning maneuvers. The noise didn't bother Sweeney a bit—in fact, he sort of liked it. The ride up to Lakenheath early that morning had taken Sweeney through a dozen or more crooked English villages, most of them built before the sixteenth century and populated with pipe-smoking, tweedy types who, to Sweeney's mind, seemed to worship not God or money or even women but dogs and outdoor plumbing. They had tradition all right, he thought, but the whole damn country was bristling with American servicemen, American hardware, a cruise missile under every damn bush. Business as usual in East Anglia.

The bellowing F15s were, to Sweeney, pleasant advertisements of America's might. Not that he was a hawk, but it was nice to know that the supercilious English appreciated American weapons as much as some bullyboy in some fourth-rate Third World nation. These, however, were opinions that Sweeney kept to himself, because his boss didn't like his fixer to beat his chest about the States. Hughie, after all, was a diplomat now.

A black airman in baggy fatigues made his way through the empty, dark officer's club lounge. Sweeney sat at the bar.

"Mr. Sweeney, sir," said the man, in an accent that could have been South Bronx or South Carolina, "Captain Bennetti says the aircraft is ready on number two, sir."

"Thanks. You tell the captain that we are just waiting for the ambassador to show. Those limey policemen outside?"

"Yessir."

"Ask their chief to come in and see me."

"Yessir."

Sweeney didn't much like dealing with the English, and he didn't much like being in England. But Hughie Coughlin was going to be President someday and Jack Sweeney was going to be there when it happened, so if Hugh was in England, Jack was right alongside him. The English could be trouble, though. When they had their official hats on they could be as prissy a collection of humorless tight-asses as you'd meet anywhere. Particularly these Diplomatic Protection Group police guys, who were always saying things like "In view of the possibilities of risk to the ambassador's person . . ." This little trip of Coughlin's to Northern Ireland had them all stirred up.

Headaches, thought Jack again, just headaches.

Commander Stubbs weaved through the tables to the bar.

"You wanted to see me, Mr. Sweeney?"

"That's right, Commander. Have a seat." He motioned to a barstool. Sweeney had heard that the DPG were pretty good, and he knew they were the only British policemen who carried guns as a matter of routine. Stubbs was a young man who looked as if he'd be good at his job, but all the same Sweeney wished he could have brought some of the Secret Service guys from the embassy.

"The ambassador should be here soon, and then we'll be getting this show on the road." Sweeney smiled at the young man, who regarded him coolly.

To Stubbs, Sweeney looked like a caricature of an Irish-American politician, with his big belly covered by an extravagant waistcoat, his steel-gray hair, and his huge, tufted eyebrows.

"It's only fair to warn you that the ambassador will be making a statement in Belfast that your government will welcome, and which will be viewed with extreme disfavor by certain elements in Northern Ireland." And which will lose us half a million votes in New York alone when Hughie runs for President, thought Sweeney.

Stubbs had no doubt who the "certain elements" were.

"I don't suppose . . ." Stubbs began.

". . . that I could tell you what he's going to say," Sweeney finished for him. "I'm afraid I can't. But it's going to make your job a lot tougher when he's through saying it."

A siren could be heard above the roar of the jets. "Sounds like the ambassador made it," said Sweeney.

"I'm sure, Mr. Sweeney, that we shall be equal to anything certain elements might be planning to do, if they plan anything at all."

"I'm sure you are, Commander," said Sweeney with a smile, suppressing the desire to call the young man Stubbsie.

Jack Sweeney thought that Hugh Coughlin's trip to Ulster was similar to campaigning in the Irish neighborhoods of New York City. Red-faced ladies kissed Coughlin a lot and their equally red-faced husbands jostled one another in an attempt to shake his hand.

They heard some Irish music performed by young men in Levi's and Aran sweaters, and watched some dances by little girls so pretty and so serious that it made Sweeney want to laugh out loud. The Protestant leaders were polite—they reminded Sweeney of Republican congressmen from Tuxedo Park and Fishkill—but aloof, afraid that Coughlin had come to their city just to grandstand a little.

Stubbs's men used a foolproof method to avoid any incidents. No itinerary for Coughlin's movements had been published—indeed, one did not exist. After an official function Coughlin would be whisked away to a site chosen at random only minutes before, to meet the people in the street. The system worked well and surprised and delighted the Belfasters, who, coming out of a supermarket, would find themselves face to face with the famous, glamorous Hugh Coughlin.

People did express disappointment that Jennifer hadn't been able to join him.

"What's the matter, sir," asked one old man, "don't you trust us?"

46

"No," said Coughlin, laughing, "Irishmen are so charming I was afraid I would be going back to London alone."

A few young men on the edge of the crowd looked a little menacing, and Stubbs's men watched them carefully, waiting to pounce if they made anything approaching a threatening gesture. But all they did was shout, "Hughie, help us get the Brits out!" which Coughlin diplomatically pretended not to have heard.

"I have a cousin in New York," said one young woman, seizing Coughlin by the arm. "His name is Seamus O'Toole."

"Well, why don't you go over to New York and see him?" said Coughlin, laughing again. "I'm sure he'd be glad to see a pretty girl like you."

Standing on the steps of the City Hall in Donegal Square, Coughlin made a short speech. "I'm speaking here today," he said, "not to the citizens of Belfast, but to the citizens of my own country. Well-intentioned Americans of Irish descent send money to this country. Money meant not to build but to fund destruction. Not to promote harmony, but to foster dissent. . . ."

Good-bye, Jackson Heights, thought Jack Sweeney Good-bye, South Boston. . . .

"It is well known," continued Coughlin, "that the money used by the many bloodstained factions in Northern Ireland comes from the United States. As a human being, I abhor this pointless waste of lives. But worse, as an American with the blood of generations of Ulstermen in my veins, I am ashamed. . . ."

Suddenly the smiles vanished. That night in The Lewis and in The Foyles and in a dozen different pubs in the Falls Road, the drinkers would say that Hughie Coughlin let them down. In Protestant Ulster, they would say that it was about time someone talked sense.

Jack Sweeney looked rather mournful on the flight back to Lakenheath.

Coughlin tried to cheer him up. "It had to be said, Jack."

"I suppose," said Sweeney.

"Cheer up. No one will remember when the time comes. We'll win, you'll see."

In The Lewis, just before closing, Billy Hanlon said, "The shame of it is that Coughlin will be President someday, and we'll get no support from him."

"If he lives that long," said Denny the barman.

CHAPTER
FIVE

Charlie Leary was getting a bit sick of this. Scotland was bloody cold, the work was bloody hard, he hadn't had a drop in six weeks, and this Jones and his mate Flynn were fucking bastards. Run up the hill. Run down the hill. Up the hill again, then back down again. Then up again. Down again. All the time shifting that bloody pitchfork tied to his back and Jones or Flynn or both of them down at the bottom of the hill with a stopwatch and sour expressions.

Six times up and down, and Leary dropped at their feet in the cold grass, lungs bursting, the strap holding the pitchfork to his back cutting into his cold sweaty flesh. He panted for a moment and stared at the two pairs of combat boots.

"He's not fast enough, Mr. Flynn," said Mr. Jones.

"You're right, Mr. Jones, not fast enough."

"Sod off," Leary moaned into the grass.

Flynn nudged him with his boot. "Off you go, Leary. Make an effort this time."

"No," said Leary, "it's not worth it."

"Well, Mr. Flynn, what do you make of that?"

"No sense of duty. No sense of the cause."

"Sod the cause," said Leary.

"The trouble with Mr. Leary, Mr. Flynn," said Mr. Jones, "is that he doesn't appreciate how lucky he is."

"There you're right, Mr. Jones."

"I think we should teach him to appreciate the finer things in life...."

"Such as, Mr. Jones?"

"Shoes, Mr. Flynn."

Leary raised his head. His carrot-colored hair was matted about his ears and neck by sweat and the damp on the ground. He stared at the two men for a moment, Flynn a bantamweight, small but wiry, with a face as obviously Irish as his accent; Jones, pig-eyed and malevolent, thickset, with ginger hair going dirty and a bottle-brush mustache. They stared back down at Leary, Flynn smiling slightly. Leary looked out over the barren Scottish landscape. He didn't even know where the hell he was, there wasn't a soul for miles, just wind, water, and heather. He shifted his gaze to the hill, examining the stiff grass and shale that littered the slopes. These two crazy buggers wanted him to run across that lot without his shoes on. Leary suddenly longed for the drab, bombed-out Falls Road.

"You're barmy," he said.

"The choice is yours, Mr. Leary," said Jones.

"Why do I have to do all this running?" Leary whined. "I thought I had to kill some fella."

"Speed," said Jones professorially, "will be your best weapon. When the time comes, Leary, my lad, you'll have to move fast. The whole bleeding world is going to be after you once you've pulled the trigger, and we don't want you getting yourself caught."

"What about the shooting?"

"That'll be the easy part," said Flynn. "Your target will be trapped and won't be shooting back. It will be as easy as watering the garden with a hose. It's once the shooting stops that you'll have to start worrying."

"So get moving," said Jones, nudging Leary with the toe of his boot.

Groaning, Leary got to his feet and stumbled toward the slope, unsteady, like a cow prodded off a road by a farmer.

"Pick it up, Leary," bellowed Flynn.

Leary stepped up his pace.

"Coming along nicely," said Flynn when Leary was out of earshot.

"Never would have believed it," said Jones.

When he had been told that Leary was the man they needed he had been dubious. Leary was a braggart, a drinker, too violent and too stupid for the sensitive task at hand. But Flynn had explained it carefully. Leary thought enough of himself to take on the job, he was violent enough to pull it off, and he was stupid enough to do as he was told. It was, Jones realized later, a surprisingly good piece of man management.

Leary's legs worked independent of his brain, his limbs alone realizing that the faster they carried him to the top of the hill, the faster he could get down. It had all looked so easy a few weeks earlier. Belfast had been getting on his nerves, the chances for petty crime were dwindling as army control tightened. Leary needed money, and in a pathetic sort of way, he was yearning for self-respect. He had been closed out of the Brotherhood years ago. They wouldn't even consider him.

Then along came Flynn.

"We need you now, Charlie," he had said. "We've got something big planned and you're the man that can do it."

Leary kept running and hocked up some phlegm on the grass.

He had almost told them to go fuck themselves. *We* need *you.* *He* had never needed *them.*

Then Flynn had told him a bit more: "We need someone the Brits don't know. Someone cold. Someone who hasn't got his prints and pictures plastered all over their files. Someone who has kept himself clean but wouldn't object to a little dirty work.... And Charlie, my boy, this is big. Bloody big...." They had been sitting in a pub at the time and because Flynn was buying, Leary had ordered himself another whiskey, a double.

After a sip, Leary asked, "How big?"

"The biggest." Flynn had smiled.

"Who?"

"No names yet, Charlie. You won't know till the day before. It's safer that way."

"But I'm going after someone important?"

"Yes, lad." Flynn had thought to himself, Another bloke trying to prove how nasty he was, another side-pocket Hitler.

"Bigger than Mountbatten?"

"Twice the size and twice as grand, Charlie. It's a one-shot deal. You give us a hand now and we'll never bother you again. We'll train you, equip you . . . and when the struggle is over we'll name a street after you."

Then the icing: Flynn mentioned payment. "Five thousand pounds, all yours."

"And I'll have learnt myself a trade," Leary had said, laughing and helping himself to another of Flynn's whiskies.

He reached the top of the hill and looked down at the two men waiting for him on the plain. Leary unslung the pitchfork and looked down the shaft as if it were a gun. His chest heaved from his run and it was hard to hold the heavy implement steady.

"After the job, whoever the bastard is," he whispered, "I'll come back and get you two. . . ."

From below Flynn and Jones watched their charge.

"He's plotting his revenge," said Flynn, smiling.

"Stupid wanker," said Jones. "I'll give 'im revenge."

Shepherd Market does not look like a red-light district and, furthermore, is not in a section of London where one is likely to be found. In these quiet streets a stroller will find none of the trappings that usually surround commercial sex: no pornographic bookstores, no massage parlors, and, once the few pubs in the area close, hardly any street life at all. Shepherd Market is in Mayfair, the most expensive and most elite of London's neighborhoods. Within a few blocks of Shepherd Market's quiet streets are London's finest hotels, its most expensive shops, its most exclusive clubs. Nearby are several Royal residences, including Buckingham Palace itself; the number could be increased if one were willing to include as "Royal Homes" the residences of a half dozen monarchs without nations who are living out their lives in genteel obscurity within the opulent confines of Mayfair, spending the treasuries of countries that no longer exist.

Paying for sex is not illegal in Britain, but this does not mean that prostitution is legal. While payment is perfectly aboveboard, asking for payment—or having someone, a pimp, say, ask for you—is not. To circumvent this legal wrinkle, a London prostitute will advertise in a discreet way. Next to the doorbells of most Shepherd Market doorways the sharp-eyed observer will see tiny signs: YOUNG MODEL, 2ND FLOOR; ANNETTE, PLEASE COME UP. (Names in Shepherd Market, as in Soho, follow a pattern. Here French names—Colette, Sophie, Lucille—predominate.)

It was another wet and cold night, and after three, a time when most of the tiny lights over the French names had been turned out. He walked, not from name to name, weighing Marie against Mimi, but directly to a doorway near Trebeck Street and rang the doorbell marked Françoise. Without waiting for a ring in reply—he knew she was free—he walked the two flights of narrow stairs and knocked at the door on the landing. It was opened quickly. He was to be Françoise's last client of the evening and she wanted to get this over with.

Françoise was pretty enough, but tired. She faked a smile for him.

"You're up late," she said.

Just inside the door he stood woodenly and remembered what the first girl had said.

"I couldn't sleep," he said.

"Well, come in, make yourself cozy." She brushed against him, the damp on his raincoat reaching her skin through the light dressing gown she wore.

"Horrible weather," she said, closing the door.

"Yes."

Before she slipped out of her robe she wondered which type

of client she hated more: the type that acted as if he owned the place or the ones like him, who looked as if they were about to wet their pants. As it happened, she never had a chance to make up her mind.

Stretched naked on his bed Tony Pidgeon poured himself the last of a bottle of Bisquit and stared at his stomach. The vista displeased him. In the army it had been flat and hard, but now, while he was not as paunchy as some of the blokes in Division, a hint of fat, of spread, was beginning to show under the orderly line of hair that ran from his navel to his crotch. It was not, as he well knew, the result of easy living and good food— he didn't really know where it came from. He searched his woozy mind. Too much boozing, he told himself, employing the emphatics of a drunk. Brandy drinking was a rotten, expensive habit he had picked up in the service and it was a habit that died hard. Maybe it was an addiction. He was drunk on a Tuesday night with a full day's work ahead of him tomorrow. What a chump. He threw an arm over his eyes.

"Bugger all," he said aloud.

Over the years he had built up a considerable reservoir of resentment, a pool that overflowed its banks when he had had too much. Where the resentment came from and against exactly what or whom it was directed he couldn't say. His father had always called him a vengeful little shaver, sometimes in pride (when an eight-year-old Tony Pidgeon had punched up an older, stronger school-yard bully), sometimes in annoyance (when Pidgeon at sixteen had thumped a barman who had refused to serve him, even though he was underage). Now his resentment sprayed out like scattershot. He resented the department, his life, even himself—everything, it seemed, had made him into a humorless tough guy with no place to go and who was expected to go quietly. He resented not having the things he wanted and the people who had them—not because they were better than he, but because they were richer, or more powerful, or spoke correctly, or went to the right schools.

54

It had been worse as a constable. He'd caution some Oxford moron who was trying to drive his Ferrari on the pavement, and then have to bash some little bastard from Brixton for nicking a bottle from an Off-License. He had hoped that plainclothes would be different, and it was. Now, instead of walking a beat and taking presents from shopkeepers at Christmastime or turning a blind eye when an M.P. was caught in a punch-up with his boyfriend, he just sat quiet, doing his time, waiting. . . . The trouble was, he didn't know what he was waiting for. He'd be Smudge Huddleston in fifteen years or, worse, big Alf Hartley, who had to laugh at everything or he'd break down crying.

It had been more of the Pomeroy case that day. The lab reports had come back four days late, and apart from a single interesting sentence (*The wounds inflicted on the body were not caused by weapons seen in street crimes of this type*—"So it wasn't a kitchen knife," Alf had said. "Why can't they say so?"), there had not been a damn thing to go on. He had spoken to all of the policemen who had been on duty in Soho that night, and they reported nothing unusual. Pidgeon had a feeling he knew why—it had been a bloody cold, wet night and most of the coppers had probably been off warming their bums someplace.

He sipped his brandy and convinced himself that it tasted good. He continued to stare moodily at his navel. A slow, silly smile spread across his face and he waved at his penis.

"Hello," he said, as if he were talking to a neighbor over a back fence. "Haven't sent you much business lately."

The momentary lightness passed as he finished his drink and he closed his eyes. He had not intended to go to sleep—he had things to sort out—but despite himself his mind made that slow fade to gray, followed a few seconds later, it seemed, by the ringing of the telephone. Pidgeon awoke instantly, unsure of where he was or indeed if it was day or night. Instinct drove him in the direction of the telephone and instinct told him what it meant.

"Did I wake you?" said Smudge.

Pidgeon cleared his throat and tried—as if there were some shame to being caught sound asleep at 4:00 a.m.—to sound wide-awake. "It's okay," he said amiably, mainly because friendliness was the only response he could think of at the moment.

"We've got another one."

"Oh?" said Pidgeon. "Same bloke?"

" 'Fraid so."

The bastard, thought Pidgeon. He sounded wide-awake. "Where?"

"Shepherd Market; 14 Trebeck Street."

"You there already?"

"I'm on my way."

"Listen," said Pidgeon, "can you send a car for me?"

"Can't do that," said Huddleston, and hung up.

As soon as Pidgeon's feet hit the floor he knew he was still drunk. His legs and fingers felt numb, and his head felt as if it had ballooned to twice its size. A buzz like a sixty-cycle hum from a fluorescent light motored through his brain. He got up, turned on the shower cold and hard, but before getting in he ran to the kitchen. He scooped the coffee pot off the stove, breaking a glass that stood on the draining board as he did so, although in his fuddled state he hardly noticed. He could feel the weight of at least a cup of the nearly twenty-four-hour-old coffee in the pot. He turned on the heat under it and walked back to the bathroom. As he stepped under the shower, standing under the frigid water like a statue in a fountain, a voice at the back of his brain told him that he was going through all this for Smudge Huddleston's benefit. God, how he hated that man.

The effort hadn't really done any good. Pidgeon looked like a corpse when he arrived at 14 Trebeck Street. Smudge stood in the center of the room as stretcher men and photographers coaxed what was left of Françoise into a body bag or onto film. It was not the sight of the woman's body—which was hard to identify as a body unless you looked at it closely—that caused Pidgeon's stomach to shift like a ship in a rough sea but Huddleston's pipe tobacco. It was cheap and sweet and stung Pidgeon's nostrils.

"Hullo, Tony," said a photographer. "You look horrible."

Pidgeon wanted to say something really nasty but couldn't think of anything. He just smiled weakly. "What've we got?" he managed to ask.

"Repeat. Same bloke," said Smudge, drawing on his pipe. "Only this time we were close to him."

"Who found the body?"

"The fire brigade."

"Funny, Smudge," said Pidgeon, feeling the urge to ram Huddleston's cheap briar down his throat.

"I'm serious," said Smudge; "999 got a call for the Mayfair Brigade for a fire at this address at three-seventeen. They didn't find any fire, but they did find our Françoise here."

Pidgeon wished he had taken a longer shower. "The false alarm was our man?"

"It stands to reason."

"Were they recording?"

"They're checking that."

Pidgeon shook his head to clear it. "Why would he call the fire brigade?"

"He didn't want a repeat of the three-day lag in the Pomeroy murder."

"Right," said Pidgeon dully. "Why, do you think?"

"Likes to have his name in the papers," said Smudge.

Pidgeon rubbed his eyes, which hurt from brandy and lack of sleep. "Why not call the police?"

"Gives him more time to get away," said Smudge evenly. He had thought it all through while Pidgeon was in the shower.

Pidgeon kicked himself. Of course, he bleeding knew that. But Smudge was scoring off him every time he opened his mouth. He hated him just a little bit more.

"Anyone see anything?"

"No," said Smudge, "nobody saw a bloody thing."

"Hear anything?"

"What do you think?" asked Smudge, looking Pidgeon square in his bloodshot eyes.

"Nothing, right?"

"That's right."

"Fancy a kidney?" said a member of the medical team, cheerfully holding one of Françoise's in a pair of tongs. He had pulled it from under the bed.

"Oh, bloody hell," said Pidgeon wearily.

Sir Randolph Astley sipped his cup of tea and scanned the television page of *The Times.*

It is popularly thought that prominent British civil servants, the mandarins of Whitehall, have more than their share of secret vices and perversions; the iconography of British satire includes such stock characters as riotously homosexual officers of the better regiments, flagellant judges, pederastic lords. Randolph Astley, a retiring man with a placid façade as smooth as the smiling face of a Buddha, couldn't vouch for the vices of his peers, but he could ruefully admit to one of his own, a vice he considered so vile that he would have died rather than have it revealed. He loved, he was addicted to, he could not live without American television programs.

He carefully read *The Times* "Personal Choice" television column. For that evening *The Times* critic was recommending a documentary about Baluchistan, a show about the training of sheepdogs, and a television play about a family of dock workers. Sir Randolph shook the paper in annoyance.

"Snobs," he said under his breath.

"More tea, Sir Randolph?" asked Hatton, Astley's aging manservant.

"Yes, please, Hatton."

Sir Randolph's devotion to the much-derided American television shows was absolute. He never missed an episode of *Dallas, Soap, The Streets of San Francisco,* or *Knots Landing.* Privately he had mourned deeply the passing of *Starsky and Hutch.* But that cloud contained a decidedly silver lining: *Starsky and Hutch* had been replaced with a show that fast became Sir Randolph's favorite, *The Dukes of Hazzard.* Week after week he'd sit in his study crouched over his television set, the red-neck soundtrack of *The Dukes* turned low, absorbing with the air of a believer every word uttered by the Duke boys and Boss Hogg, and drinking in the feline movements of Miss Daisy, watching fascinated and wide-eyed as the cars so expertly piloted by the Dukes careened along the back roads of Hazzard County. The Dukes were a startling contrast to the dukes Sir Randolph knew. He preferred Bo and Luke.

He sighed as he put aside his newspaper and began steeling himself for the ordeal of another day. Years of working with royalty had taught Sir Randolph that crowned heads were, for the most part, rather ordinary people. In truth, he didn't really like them, and George was no exception. He didn't care for many people, when it came right down to it, except for raucous television stars. It bothered him to think that his idols would probably not care for him in the least.

Royals were so earnest, Sir Randolph reflected, so deeply concerned—if only for a short time—with the tasks toward which they were directed by some soft-handed servant like himself. The Royal Family works for me, Sir Randolph told himself with pleasure, and they do as they're told.

At nine-fifteen Hatton asked the same question he did every morning: "Would you like me to call the car, Sir Randolph?"

And as always Sir Randolph replied: "Nine-fifteen already, Hatton?"

And every morning Hatton thought the same thing: No, it's half past my arsehole, poncy.

Sunk in the backseat of his Daimler, Sir Randolph watched the hordes of office workers streaming from the Green Park tube station into the cold morning and reflected, as he often did, that he was glad that he had money. The guards at the palace presented arms as his car passed, and the constable on duty at the gate saluted as his Daimler swept across the palace forecourt. The car drove through the front courtyard and stopped in front of a porte cochere. A two-minute walk through the east wing and Sir Randolph entered his office. It was nine-thirty and yesterday's dispatch boxes had been neatly stacked on his desk for his review, before they would be returned to the appropriate government departments. He felt like a first-form teacher going over the night's homework, deleting any questions that George had asked that Sir Randolph felt the King would be better off not having answered. Pruning, he called it.

He glanced at the morning's mail. A letter, obviously constructed laboriously with a copy of *Debrett's* at the writer's side, invited HRH the King to the opening of a new abattoir in Bristol. Sir Randolph liked to schedule George for a really awful appointment every so often—the "filthies," he called them—and the opening of a slaughterhouse would do nicely. In neat precise letters at the bottom of the letter he wrote "Accept."

CHAPTER
SIX

If a crime is not solved in the first twenty-four hours, chances are that it will not be solved at all. Probably the best-known piece of police lore going, Pidgeon reflected, also absolutely true. He stirred his milky, sweet tea absently and did a bit of mental arithmetic. Françoise (also known as Marjorie Stewart, he now knew) had been discovered at 3:23 a.m. It was now—he glanced at the clock hanging on the wall—9:56 a.m. He and Smudge had about sixteen hours of their allotted twenty-four to catch Jack. He sipped his tea, and realized that they hadn't a prayer.

The Scotland Yard canteen was as warm and inviting as a railway station, although at that moment the Ritz Grill would not have cheered Pidgeon. He had been up all night and had accomplished nothing since, but already the night seemed a few centuries behind him. Smudge came over to his table and methodically laid a place for himself, knife, fork, spoon across the top to form a three-sided square, as if he were expecting the vicar for tea. In the midst of the cutlery he placed a plate of bacon and eggs, and sat down.

"That's your second breakfast today," said Pidgeon.

"Hungry," said Huddleston, fighting a stringy bit of bacon. "The other one was hours ago."

The two men sat and did not speak for a while. Only the deep, mouthy click of Smudge's false teeth broke the silence. Pidgeon looked around him. On the bulletin board were the few standard notices: blood drives, police athletics. A sign announced VICE SQUAD OUTING TO CALAIS.

"What's next?" asked Pidgeon, not so much for the information as to cover the Morse code issuing from Smudge's mouth.

"Finish my breakfast and then see if I can't catch forty winks someplace." Smudge looked as if he could use it.

"And what about our new corpse?"

Smudge put down his knife and fork. "What would you do?"

Pidgeon surrendered the point, shrugging his shoulders. Briefly, he considered putting in for a transfer. "You've given up, haven't you?"

Smudge wiped his mouth. "I haven't," he said evenly. "I just can't make up my mind what to do next. I think it needs thinking on. . . ." He delicately heaped some cold egg yolk onto a finger of toast. "Have you been upstairs? The postman has come."

Pidgeon shook his head. "No. Don't tell me there's more. . . ."

"'Fraid so," said Smudge.

"Christ! Shit! I can't even find my phone. . . ."

"Language," cautioned Smudge.

Since the killing of Brenda Pomeroy, both Pidgeon and Huddleston had come to dread the two daily visits of the mail carts. At first it was an office joke. "There's nothing like a good murder to bring out the loonies," Alf Hartley observed. But now the mountains of letters—theories, confessions, accusations—had become a monumental annoyance. They were stacked across both desks, on the floor, on the filing cabinets. A piece of paper with, say, an essential phone number could vanish into the swamp of dirty envelopes and be gone for good.

Pidgeon had complained to Hartley as soon as it became apparent that the avalanche of letters was to become a twice-a-day occurrence.

Hartley had only smiled. "Sorry, Tony, I'd like to give you more staff, but I just haven't got it."

"What about Harris? Or Donaldson? Or MacWilliams?"

"They're busy," said Hartley, turning away. But Pidgeon pursued him.

"Like hell they're busy! Harris has been working on the GBH number in Victoria for a month. . . ."

To Pidgeon's surprise, Hartley became very angry. "Get off my back, Tony! You copped this case—if the work is too much for you, then too bloody bad. Don't come whining to me every time you feel put upon. . . . Get someone else to change your bleeding nappies."

Tony had gone white with anger during the tirade. "All right," he said, "take me off the case."

Hartley looked at him long and hard. "Not bloody likely," he muttered.

No one could talk to Pidgeon for the rest of the day. Unless, as Harris pointed out, you wanted to lose a finger or two.

Unexpectedly, peace was restored when Hartley managed to get two constables assigned to take up the slack during night duty. It wasn't much, but it made a difference.

Secretly, Huddleston worried about the lack of cooperation that they encountered with Hartley. Rare was the murder investigation that didn't have at least four men assigned to it right off the bat. Of course, it was no secret that no one really cared about a tom killer, except the press, of course. Let Jack kill a civilian—then a proper case would be started. Huddleston wondered idly if he would be allowed to lead it. Unlikely, he thought.

The letters were sorted into four piles: Maybe, Not Likely, Confession, and Cuckoo. The Cuckoo pile dwarfed the other three. The two men sat side by side, slitting the letters open, glancing at them, discarding them. Both fell into a maddeningly similar rhythm.

"Precision," said Alf, faking admiration, "like finely balanced timepieces."

"More like occupational therapy," said Lennie Harris, a sergeant, "like loonies making wallets."

As the day progressed Pidgeon and Huddleston found their attentions divided between the telephone and the letters. On the phone were the gentlemen of the press: Were they close to making an arrest? (No comment); Was there a motive? (No); Was it true that the fire brigade had found the body? (Yes); Was Jack expected to strike again? (No comment). The switchboard managed to screen most of the crank calls, but a few got through. Pidgeon was particularly adept at handling these— Huddleston would get hung up on the phone for hours listening to convoluted theories postulated by a retired railway worker or a curate in Manchester: the Ripper was doing God's work (Interesting angle); the Ripper was doing Satan's work (We gathered). A number of prostitutes called in, some scared and pleading (For God's sake, catch him. We're terrified). Others scared and belligerent (You bastards won't do a thing till he kills a "good girl").

So the day passed. As the evening papers went to press, the phone stopped ringing, but the mail remained as daunting as ever.

Pidgeon opened a letter.

"Dear Sir, I am the reincarnation of S. Holmes, detective." Cuckoo.

"Dear Superintendent Pidgeon, I have had a vision of evil. . . ." Cuckoo.

Huddleston opened a letter, noticed that it had been sent "From Hell" and turned to drop it on its proper pile, then stopped. He leaned back in his chair, holding the letter in front of him.

"Tony."

"What?" He slashed an envelope without looking up.

"Listen to this one: 'I am at large and down on whores. There's plenty of time for me to do my work, and I shall see that I am not disturbed. Catch me if you can, Mr. Lusk. Jack.' "

"Mister who?" said Pidgeon without much interest, his eyebrows knitting together. "Put it in the Confession pile." All the confessions would later be sorted by postmark and dispatched to the CID office covering that district. A few of the letters had return addresses and their senders would receive visits from uniformed police constables. It was strictly routine.

"I think we're going about this all wrong," said Huddleston, a note of conviction in his voice.

Pidgeon cast a letter aside and silently complained to himself: Agatha Christie again.

"You don't know who Mr. Lusk is, do you?"

"Lusk?" said Pidgeon, staring at the fluorescent light. "No, I don't."

"He was involved in the original investigation team. I don't think he was a copper. He was head of a citizens' committee—I forget the name."

"Original investigation?"

"The first Jack the Ripper. In 1888."

Pidgeon ran his hand through his hair. "So?"

"I've read a book or two on the original case and this letter is just like one sent to Lusk. I don't think it's exactly the same, but it sounds familiar. I remember thinking what an odd name Lusk was."

"I don't see the point." Pidgeon glanced out the window at the gray, rain-pelted day.

"Well, this letter, here," Smudge continued with the air of a professor, "which is from some nut case in"—he glanced at the postmark—"Eastbourne, has told us something."

"Oh, yes? What's that?"

"Well, we've been calling this bloke Jack the Ripper, right?"

Pidgeon sighed. "Right."

"But we've just been calling him that because he's some nana that goes around attacking prostitutes with a knife."

"Seems fair."

"No," said Smudge. "We've come to call anyone who commits that type of crime Jack the Ripper. But our bloke actually *thinks* he's Jack the Ripper."

"Smudge, what are you on about?"

Huddleston grasped Pidgeon by the forearm. "Don't you see? These are reenactments. We think he has left hardly a trace behind. But he has—the crimes themselves."

"A dead giveaway, that is."

"In the original Ripper crimes," said Smudge patiently, "nobody heard or saw anything. The police never had any leads. The crimes were committed with an unidentifiable knife, something out of the ordinary. Pieces of the victims were removed, internal organs—all true in the case of our two victims."

"I see your point, Smudge. But it's thin. . . ."

"Our suspect is someone who would have a profound knowledge of the Ripper crimes," said Huddleston.

"You've got a profound knowledge of the Ripper crimes, Smudge. There have been hundreds of books, films . . . it's not exactly a secret how he operated."

"The more we know about the original crimes the more we'll know about our man," said Smudge.

"And we'll never find him," said Pidgeon crossly.

"Got a present for you," said Lennie Harris, dropping a small packet onto Pidgeon's desk.

"What's this?"

"Came in the departmental post."

Pidgeon tore open the wrapper. It was a cassette from the 999 exchange, a recording of the voice that reported the fire that morning at Trebeck Street. A note attached said that the original tape was undergoing voice analysis and prints at the lab.

For the first time that day, Pidgeon felt a lift. "This is something," he said, waving the tape at Huddleston.

Alf Hartley kept a cassette player in his office, a glassed-in corner of the room. Pidgeon led the way, with Smudge just behind.

————

The day was winding down and Alf and a few of the lads were telling jokes in his office. Hartley smiled broadly at Pidgeon. "Tony, old son ..."

"Listen, Alf—"

"What's the definition of a perfect woman?"

"Listen, Alf, I've got something."

"Someone who fucks all night and at midnight turns into a pint and a ham sandwich."

Lennie Harris laughed and so did Hartley. Pidgeon had not been listening. Smudge had, and did not approve.

"What?" said Pidgeon.

"Sorry, Smudge," said Hartley.

Pidgeon went on talking, waving the tape. "Listen, Alf, we've got a tape of the bloke who reported the fire this morning."

"Oh, very nice," said Hartley. "Let's have a listen."

A short breathy hiss came through the speaker, followed by the voice of the operator.

"What service, please?"

"Fire brigade."

Pidgeon stared at the speaker of the tape recorder. The voice was quiet, calm, educated, and ageless. The tape had a slightly hollow sound, provided no doubt by the glassed-in phone box.

"Go ahead, please."

"There is a fire at 14 Trebeck Street."

"Can you see the flames?" the operator asked with professional detachment.

There was no answer, but neither was there the sound of the connection being broken.

"Can you see the flames?"

The connection held.

"Your name, please."

Pidgeon could hear the operator thinking of what he had read in his training manual. The best way to get a name from an anonymous caller was, simply, to ask. The reaction to respond with one's name was almost automatic.

But not Jack.

The operator repeated the question. The answer was the

sound of the connection being broken.

"What do you think of that?" asked Pidgeon in the silence that followed.

"Not much," said Alf Hartley.

"Your man is from London and between the ages of twenty-five and a hundred," said Mike Donaldson, a fellow Pidgeon had never liked much.

"Smudge?"asked Hartley.

"It's a start," said Smudge uncertainly.

"The start of what?" asked Hartley.

"Listen, it's better than nothing, right?" said Pidgeon.

"And nothing is just what you've got, Tony," said Hartley. "Now clear off, I've got some work to do."

"What bit him?" asked Pidgeon as they made their way back to their desks.

"We're not doing very well," said Smudge quietly.

"We haven't had much to work with," said Pidgeon.

"Not really an excuse, is it?" said Smudge.

"Whose side are you on?"

"Just stating a fact."

The long day and the long night before it got the better of Pidgeon. "Well, just shut up."

It was very unlike him but Smudge was suddenly very angry. "Don't you talk that way to me. You keep a civil tongue in your head," he said through his teeth.

"Get lost," said Pidgeon, feeling foolish.

"Listen to me," said Huddleston, raising his voice. "I'm senior on this case and you'll not forget it."

"Senior!" Pidgeon's voice was raised just short of a shout. "You're bloody senile. You're over the hill."

The other men in the room pretended not to have heard, but exchanged smirks and glances as if Huddleston and Pidgeon were a married couple arguing at a cocktail party.

Smudge got very red in the face. "You're going to have to learn some manners, my lad."

"Manners? My lad?" said Pidgeon incredulously. "Where do you think you bloody are? In the bloody Boy Scouts?"

"All right, darlings," said Hartley, appearing in the doorway of his office. He banged the doorframe with a case book. "Wrap up."

Huddleston and Pidgeon sat down again stiff and proper at their desks. Both men seethed, angry at each other and embarrassed, like boys reprimanded in front of the whole class.

The Mortlake public library had been built in the 1950s and had grown old very quickly. It had been the grace note of a redevelopment scheme, a proud, if ordinary, piece of architecture of reinforced concrete that cracked easily and grayed like dirty linen. The library at the Yard would have suited Smudge's needs better, but he wanted to test his theory in private.

A librarian sat at a raised desk, the collar of her cardigan clipped together with a little black chain. She kept a sharp eye on some children at one of the tables who were sniggering among themselves at a reproduction of the *Venus of Urbino* hanging on the wall. She looked at Smudge as if he were a child molester.

"Crime," he said. "I'm looking for books on—"

"Fiction or nonfiction?"

"Nonfiction."

"File 17," she said, pointing toward a row of cabinets.

"Thanks," said Smudge, feeling lucky that he had gotten off so easily.

He had more than a passing knowledge of the Ripper crimes, having read a book or two on the subject over the years, and he could not escape the conclusion that the Metropolitan Police of the day had horribly botched the investigation. There was talk that they had lost or simply destroyed evidence, hushed up details of the case, and generally behaved in an unprofessional manner. There had been persistent rumors that they were covering for someone very important—

Queen Victoria's grandson, to be exact—but that had never been proved. A ridiculous idea when you thought about it, Smudge felt.

The Complete Jack the Ripper by Donald Rumbelow caught his eye. A broad overview of the crimes was exactly what Smudge needed. Without difficulty, Smudge found the book on the shelves and retreated to a vacant table. He placed a school exercise book on the table for taking notes and began to read methodically.

The first line of the second paragraph of the introduction stopped him. "One of the oddest aspects of the Ripper murders is that Victorians did not recognize them as sex crimes." Of course, Smudge thought, everyone assumed that the Pomeroy and Stewart murders were of a sexual nature, although neither had been sexually assaulted. One of these days he would be getting the police psychologist's report on the type of illness that afflicted the new Jack. He took his first note: (1) *Sex crimes.* He underlined it neatly and read on.

The dimly remembered suspects came back to him: Montague Druitt, a lonely young man, "sexually insane" according to the police, who drowned himself in the Thames; George Chapman, a Polish barber-surgeon, who poisoned his three wives; the mysterious Dr. Pedachenko, an agent of the Russian secret police; the even more mysterious Dr. Stanley, who, Rumbelow thought, never existed at all; the infamous Dr. Neill Cream, arsonist, blackmailer, abortionist, who was convicted of the murder of four whores in 1892. All were discussed and dismissed by Rumbelow.

Smudge absently took out his pipe, staring about the room, thinking about what he read.

"No smoking," hissed the librarian from her desk.

"Sorry," he mumbled, returning to his book.

In 1970, Dr. Thomas Stowell caused something of a sensation when he published in *The Criminologist* his "A Solution" to the Jack the Ripper mystery. His source material was apparently the private papers of Sir William Gull, who had been Physician Extraordinary to Queen Victoria. Throughout his article Stowell referred to his suspect only as "S." However, he dropped enough clues to show that he was pointing at HRH Prince Albert Victor ("Eddy"), Duke of Clarence and the eldest son of the future King Edward VII. When asked to confirm or deny this interpretation, Stowell would do neither, apparently on the grounds that he did not wish to embarrass the Royal Family.

Smudge remembered the furor surrounding the allegation. It had been in the papers for days.

He picked up another book; *Jack the Ripper: A History,* by Mason Hope. It seemed to be much like the Rumbelow book. It contained an authoritative essay on late-nineteenth-century London slum life, an investigation of the criminal mind, but nothing that could really help him. The dedication caught Smudge's eye: "For Noah Sinclair, who knows Jack better than anyone."

Leonard Matters's *The Mystery of Jack the Ripper* was the most disappointing of all: it was the account of Dr. Stanley, who was thought to have been nothing more than a journalist's prank.

Smudge leafed through the Rumbelow again, looking at the pictures, just thinking. Another librarian, a young one, circled the room, straightening books on the shelves and returning those books discarded on the tables to their proper places. She glanced in a disinterested way at Smudge, who was staring at his book, looking a little odd.

"You all right, sir?" she asked.

"Yes, fine," he said, closing the book over his hand. She passed by, and slowly he opened it again. Reproduced in the center of the book were a couple of the police photographs of the original victims. They were horribly mutilated; one was scarcely recognizable as ever having been a human being at all. Horrifying though they were, Smudge stared, transfixed. Both of the bodies in his case, Pomeroy and Stewart, had been given the same treatment. He snapped the book shut. The photographs made him all the more sure that his theory was right.

71

Their Jack was emulating the old Jack. He walked to the librarian's desk.

A woman ahead of him was renewing *Forever Amber*. "A lovely story," she said. "This is my fifth time reading it."

Smudge could tell that the librarian didn't like him, and it made him feel uncomfortable.

"Deviant sexual behavior," he said.

"Pardon?"

"Deviant sexual behavior," repeated Smudge.

"We are a borough library, sir," said the librarian. "We don't cater to such a specialized taste. I suggest you try a medical library."

"Yes," said Smudge, retreating once again to the card catalogues. On impulse, he looked up Noah Sinclair. *Anglo-Saxon Hierarchy* was the first title he found. *The Medieval State and Its Antecedents* was another, and *Trade with the Cinque Ports and the Levant 1220–1244* was a third. There were a dozen more, all having to do with medieval history. Except one: *Musings on Murder: Some Thoughts by an Aficionado.*

Smudge found the book and, bracing himself for a final run-in with the gorgon at the desk, checked it out.

Once safely outside the building, he read the author's biography on the back flap. It was a single sentence: "Sir Noah Sinclair is the Regius Professor of History at Oxford and an OM."

An educated man, thought Smudge with relief. Someone you could trust.

Musings on Murder was an entertaining book that Smudge found a bit hard to take. Sir Noah wrote with wit and exuberance on a subject that Huddleston had considered to be very serious for many years. In his time on the force, Smudge had never quite been able to fathom just what it was that drove one person to take another's life. He could understand certain motives, of course—the clockwork mechanics that led a jealous wife to kill an unfaithful husband or an armed robber to kill a night watchman—but he could never comprehend the passions involved. To summon up that much hate or fear or menace from within oneself seemed to him not worth the effort—there must always be a more sensible way of solving one's problems, he felt, for Smudge was a well-ordered man. That was the difference between him and Sir Noah Sinclair. Sir Noah wrote, it seemed, with a full understanding of the passion of murder; indeed, he appeared to admire it.

The first chapter in the book, "Rogues' Gallery," concerned the Chamber of Horrors at Madame Tussaud's waxworks.

"You can keep the Louvre, the Tate, the Hermitage," wrote Sir Noah; "my favorite museum is under the Marylebone Road. Here is murder, not as it is, but as we want to see it, as it ought to be. . . ."

Smudge read the essay soberly and told himself that he did not agree. He knew Madame Tussaud's well and the scenes that were his favorites were not Dr. Cream or Christie the mass murderer but the tableaux that glorified British history—Queen Elizabeth, Drake, Nelson at Trafalgar, Churchill. He moved on to the next essay.

Chapter 2, "The Stonehenge of Crime," was about Jack the Ripper.

Did Jack, one wonders, ever realize how lucky he was? His is an almost unique position in British history, to be famous, yet anonymous, to be discussed and analysed and examined time and time again, and yet to remain completely unknown. Jack is an enigma, standing today as sullen and unforgiving as he did at the end of the last century, a brooding madman whom, maddeningly, we shall never know, but shall never stop seeking.

Consider, if you will, the great men of the last century: Wellington, Palmerston, Gladstone, J. S. Mill—you could name a hundred towering figures in every field of endeavour. These were interesting men, brilliant men who changed the course of history, but not one of them lives for us today as Jack does. As men, as breathing creatures, they have been made shallow by familiarity. We know what they did with every day of their lives—what they wore, ate, drank; who their

friends were; we know their enemies, their lovers—
and how human they become because of it.

Is the Duke of Wellington an immortal? Of course,
one replies. But is he spoken of today? Do we see in
the daily papers articles entitled "Who Was the Real
Iron Duke?" His historical contribution is discussed in
the universities—with an anecdote or two thrown in
by the lecturer to keep his students awake—but we
don't really care what sort of man he was, what drove
him, what sustained him. However, we would like to
know everything, everything, mind you, about a
crazed killer of East End trollops. But because we
know nothing about him, we can only draw a single
conclusion: Jack lives. . . .

A few dirty crimes (brilliantly executed, one cannot
deny that) in a festering London slum have rendered
to Jack the immortality that has escaped the great figures of history. What irony! (To stretch a point: If
Jack had commited his crimes in his early twenties, he
could have been alive as recently as 1960. How extraordinary his life must have been, knowing, for so
long, what so many wanted to know. How great the
temptation must have been to say to his neighbor in
the saloon bar: "Guess who I am. . . .")

"Interesting book, dear?" asked Irene. She sat in her armchair by the fire, her knitting in her lap, listening to rather than
watching television. It made her happy to have Smudge home
that night. He had been going out so much on this new case. It
wasn't fair, she thought, making a man of his age run around at
all hours of the night. But Sammy wasn't a man for complaining, bless him.

"Quite interesting, yes," said Smudge, not lifting his eyes
from the page. "The author is very educated, but I'm not sure
I agree with him on certain things."

"It's healthy to hear opinions other than your own from time
to time," said Irene.

CHAPTER
SEVEN

In the weeks following the slaying of Marjorie Stewart the general public and the department itself lost interest in her demise—except for Huddleston and Pidgeon who hardly spoke to each other, their little flare-up in the office having boiled down into a hard residue of resentment, exacerbated by the virtual nonexistence of leads. Not the slightest glimmer of light showed itself in the case. Jack had disappeared into the vast London populace.

The psychologist's profile suggested that the suspect was lonely, frustrated, sexually unsatisfied—a set of problems that Pidgeon regretfully recognized having himself. The voice analysis of the tape recording brought nothing, save for the single useless fact that the sound of a refuse-collection lorry could be faintly heard in the background. Smudge spent a fruitless four days interviewing dustmen, starting with the depot serving Mayfair and moving in ever-widening circles to the outskirts of London. Of course, not one of the men he had spoken to could remember anything or anyone odd in their neighborhood that night.

Smudge gradually fell back into the habit of doing some of

the lads' typing. Pidgeon spent most of his time phrasing and rewording his request for transfer—a request he probably wouldn't file—and started leaving the office at five o'clock on the dot. He knew that in another fortnight or so the Pomeroy and Stewart cases would be pronounced "Open but suspended" and consigned to a file someplace.

Pidgeon took to stopping at his favorite pub, The Antelope, on his way home. It was warm inside and as dark as a cave lit by dim brass lamps. The room smelled of spirits and food and good fellowship. Ted, the barman, had been at his job long enough to be able to tell when a patron wanted to chat and when he wanted to be alone. Mostly, Pidgeon wanted to be left alone, but sometimes he'd chat, staying in the pub till closing time, telling a few "inside the Yard" stories to the people around the bar. Everyone would stand a round or two, tell some jokes, and go home. Curiously, it was on these cheerful, boozy nights that Pidgeon would let himself into his flat, look at the unmade bed, and feel even more alone than if he had spent the evening quietly nursing a drink at the end of the bar.

Occasionally at The Antelope he'd feel like a talk, and the bar would be empty. On one such night he found himself half relieved and rather surprised to see, of all people, Smudge Huddleston coming through the door. He got a pint from Ted and carried it to Pidgeon's side.

"Evening, Tony."

"Evening, Smudge." Both men sipped. "What are you doing here?"

"Fancied a drink."

"Come on, Smudge. You're miles from home."

"I heard you mention the place to some of the lads. Thought I might give it a go. . . ."

It was a cold November night, rainy and windy. Somehow Pidgeon couldn't imagine Smudge not wanting to get home on such a night. Huddleston wasn't the sort to stop for a beer in a pub that he had heard was quite nice.

Pidgeon smiled at Smudge. Silly old geezer. "That's not very convincing. . . ."

76

Huddleston smiled back. "I suppose not."

"So why are you here, then?"

Smudge took a long pull on his drink. "Thought it was about time we had a little chat."

Pidgeon shifted against the bar, half turning to face the older man. "Go."

"Well, Tony," said Smudge, "it's like this. . . . I've been on the force for a number of years. I'm coming up for retirement next year, and I won't be sorry, I can tell you. Of course, there are things I'll miss—it's only natural, isn't it? I can't complain, really. I'll be getting a nice pension and I'll have the added satisfaction of knowing that I've been of some use. . . ."

"Of course," said Pidgeon.

"But there's one thing that bothers me. . . ." He paused and in sign language ordered a refill for both of them.

"Ta, Smudge," said Pidgeon. "What bothers you?"

"Well, these last few years—they've been a bit difficult for me. I can't really keep up. I know you younger blokes call working with me 'granddad duty.' "

"Smudge, I . . ." said Pidgeon, coloring.

"No, it's all right, Tony, I don't mind. You sort of put your finger on it the other day when you said that I was over the hill."

"I was pissed off," said Pidgeon. "Pay it no mind."

"It was fair," said Huddleston in an understanding tone of voice. "It gave me a shock, I can tell you. I thought that no one else had noticed—I mean, it's not like all the lads pull their weight except for me. I thought I was the only one who knew that I was slipping."

"This is a tough case," said Pidgeon.

"I know that," said Huddleston eagerly. "I really want us to solve this one. You've got the time, Tony; mine has just about run out. I want to go out on top, leading a successful investigation into a big crime. They've never caught a Ripper, Tony, not the first one, not the one during the war—"

"What did they call him?"

"The Blackout Ripper."

"Charming."

"They're always too clever. I want to leave having outsmarted one. It's like a godsend being put on this case. At first I thought it was a mistake; I mean, the department doesn't think I'm past it, do they? Otherwise, they wouldn't have put me on, would they?"

"No, Smudge, they wouldn't." Pidgeon was touched. For weeks Smudge had been an embarrassment, like a mother who wore the wrong kind of hat to Sports Day. But now Pidgeon couldn't help feeling for the man, realizing that if he thought things were tough on him, they were twice as hard on Huddleston. With a resolute gesture, Pidgeon finished his drink and tapped the base of his mug on the bar.

"Don't worry, Smudgie, we'll get him," he said.

"Listen," said Smudge, moving a little closer to Pidgeon and lowering his head. "I want to ask you something else."

"I'm all ears."

"Do you think Alf is acting a bit funny about all this?"

Pidgeon sipped his drink and swallowed before answering. "He's always run an open shop, Smudge. You know that. I mean, he lets the lads have a free hand...."

"That's not quite what I mean," said Smudge. "I mean, here we are investigating terror killings and we don't get much in the way of help—practically no staff, lab reports come back late. And Alf doesn't seem very interested.... It's odd, that's all."

"He's got a fair amount on his plate," said Pidgeon, wondering why he was defending Hartley. "The whole section is a bit of a handful."

"S'pose," said Smudge.

Pidgeon straightened against the bar. "As for the matter at hand," he said, as if he were a cabinet minister, "what do we do now?"

"Any ideas?" asked Smudge

"None whatsoever," said Pidgeon. "You?"

"Well, yes," said Smudge, "I have."

"Great. Where do we start?"

"Oxford," said Smudge, unfolding a letter on the bar.
"Oxford?" Pidgeon picked up the letter.

Dear Inspector Huddleston,
  I am delighted to hear from you. Although I am only an amateur in the field of criminology, I would be honoured to assist you in any way I can. You are quite correct in assuming that I have given the original Ripper case and the new one a great deal of thought. Why don't you and your colleague come to lunch on Thursday?

Yours truly,
Noah Sinclair

The old bastard has caught me again, thought Pidgeon.

Pidgeon knew that he'd feel uncomfortable in Oxford, and starting at the train station, he did. He hadn't gone to university, and despite the palavering over the years about how the Oxford bastion was opened to all qualified comers, he still resented people who studied there.

"Lovely day for a jaunt, isn't it?" said Smudge, as they got off the train and onto a cold, dreary platform. "It's a shame we won't be able to see any of the city. It's really quite a lovely town."

Pidgeon shrugged his shoulders. Those few moments of goodwill he had summoned up in The Antelope had long since evaporated as the plan had been explained to him. Smudge had told him of Sinclair's writings, of his peculiar admiration for Jack.

"So he's interested in a murderer who was never caught and who lived a hundred years ago. So what? Waste of time, that's all."

"I'm sure he can help," said Huddleston stubbornly. "Anyway, he does know a lot about Jack."

"Smudgie," said Pidgeon desperately, "he knows about the *old* Jack. It was a hundred bloody years ago."

79

"See if I'm not right."

The waiting Bentley and driver surprised both of them.

"Inspector Huddleston? I am Glover. Sir Noah asked me to meet you."

"Well," said Huddleston, "that was very kind of him."

The two policeman got into the backseat, Smudge giving Pidgeon a look that suggested that this was "a bit of the all right." People in the station forecourt tried to peer in at them as the car pulled away.

"They think we're royalty," said Smudge gleefully. "It seems that our Sir Noah is more than an ink-stained don."

"*Your* Sir Noah," corrected Pidgeon.

The house was also something of a surprise. It was not a series of rooms in a college, or even a donnish residence on the Banbury Road or Boars Hill. It was an estate, like the ones that were advertised in the front pages of the *Country Life* back numbers that Pidgeon looked through while waiting for his dentist. Houses that boasted of "seven reception rooms, stabling for twelve, and ample room for staff."

"Money," said Smudge knowingly, tapping the side of his nose.

The car pulled up next to a broad sweep of stone steps at the top of which, very far off it seemed, was the front door. The driver tried to get out in time to open Smudge's door, but Huddleston beat him to it.

"Thanks," he said. "I can manage."

Pidgeon ignored the driver and looked up at the door. Standing there was a woman smoking a cigarette. His first impression of her—he couldn't quite make out her features—was of long legs and pale skin and blond hair in loose curls falling to her shoulders. It was the kind of hair he had seen and admired on the heads of smart women on Bond Street.

"Which one of you is Inspector Huddleston?" she asked.

"I am, miss," said Smudge, climbing the steps. "We've come to see Sir Noah . . . your father?"

"My husband," she said. "Don't apologize, I'm used to it."

"May I present Sergeant Pidgeon?" said Smudge, to recover.

"I'm Margaret Sinclair," she said, shaking hands.

"Pleased to meet you," said Pidgeon. She had a narrow, brittle voice which turned each syllable finely, as if on a lathe. She sized Pidgeon up in a glance. He caught the look and wondered, as he always did, what women were thinking when they looked him over.

"My husband's in the library," she said, leading them into the house and through an entrance hall that had the proportions of a squash court.

Pidgeon watched her slim hips as they moved under her loose-fitting slacks and told himself that she looked all right with him, thanks. He glanced at Huddleston, who wasn't watching his hostess or even taking in the opulence of his surroundings. Smudge hadn't even noticed how cold it was in the house—they could see their breath. Huddleston's eyes were bright, Pidgeon realized, with the anticipation of meeting Sir Noah Sinclair, Smudge's savior, the man who might be able to breathe some life into the moribund investigation. Poor old fart.

The library, warmed by a blaze in the colossal fireplace, was packed floor to ceiling with bookshelves that had little ladders running on tracks along the walls, a half dozen painted muses looked down from the ceiling with fatuous expressions as they plucked their lyres and disported. Polyhymnia was partially obscured by a damp stain that looked as if it had been there for a century. Behind a desk at the end of the room, Sir Noah Sinclair sat enthroned.

"Here's Inspector Huddleston, darling," said Margaret, and left the room.

"Sir Noah," said Smudge, "allow me to say that this is a very great honor for me."

"Good. For me, too," said Sinclair. He did not get up. Instead, he motored out from behind the desk in an electric wheelchair.

Pidgeon was relieved to see Sir Noah so disabled. It meant that his wife's sex life was probably a bit dim. She was too young for him anyway—she couldn't have been much over thirty. Sinclar was sixty-five if he was a day.

"And you, of course, are Sergeant Pidgeon," said Sinclair.

"That's right, sir," said Pidgeon, with a false smile.

Sinclair executed an adroit two-point turn and with surprising speed headed for a couch and two armchairs in front of the fireplace.

"Sit," he ordered. "Drink?"

"No thank you, sir," said Huddleston.

"Of course," said Sinclair. "I forgot. On Duty." He had a way of speaking that rendered the first letter of certain words in capital letters. Pidgeon found it annoying. Sinclair poured himself a drink from a decanter on a tray and drove back across the room. He looked to Pidgeon as if he were a very expensive mechanical toy.

"Well," said Sinclair, "you haven't been doing terribly well, have you?"

"No, sir," said Smudge dutifully.

Fuck you, thought Pidgeon.

"I mean it in no condemnatory way," said Sinclair. "It's just a fact, rather an obvious one at that. I mean, you would hardly be likely to come chasing all the way up here to get the opinion of an old cripple if you had anything concrete to go on, would you?" Sinclair answered his own question. "Of course not."

Sinclair was white-haired and balding, with green eyes hidden under tufted white eyebrows. His shoulders were broad and strong. He was dressed casually in a light-colored shirt and a dark jacket; a plaid rug was thrown over his lap and knees. His eyes twinkled as if he were enjoying a private joke. Pidgeon had no doubt that he found them very amusing.

"So. How can I be of assistance?"

"Well," said Smudge, leaning forward in his chair. "We, rather I was wondering—" He searched his mind for the little prepared speech he had made up on the train. He couldn't find it. "I'll start again," he said.

Sinclair regarded Huddleston, all ears, while Pidgeon examined Euterpe on the ceiling.

"As you have no doubt read in the papers," said Smudge, marshaling his thoughts, "the man we're looking for has left us little to go on. There hasn't been a breath of a lead—"

"Hmm," said Sinclair, his chin sinking to his chest.

"Except for a single fact that we have noticed. Jack is consciously emulating his forebear. Some things have changed, of course, because the city has changed. The murders aren't happening in Whitechapel anymore—it's a different type of district now, and our Jack has to take his prey where he can find it."

"That's all very well," said Sinclair, "but how do I interest you?" He spoke with the air of a man who would rather talk about himself than anything else.

"Well," said Huddleston, "we feel that you might review the details with us and see how they compare with the original crime, tell us what matches and what doesn't."

"I, Inspector?" asked Sinclair modestly. "The details of the case are readily available to you, of all people. I'm just a professor of history, medieval history at that. Surely you can compare the two cases without my assistance."

"We're newcomers in the Ripper field, Sir Noah. But according to what I've read, you've been thinking about this matter for quite a while."

"Yes," said Sir Noah, "that is true. I've always intended to write a book but"—he sipped his drink—"who has the time?"

"That's a shame, sir," said Huddleston.

"Furthermore, I am an amateur." Sinclair put a slight French backspin on the word. "Surely your superiors wouldn't sanction any aid I might be able to render."

"Oh," said Pidgeon brightly, "they don't know we're here. Our super thinks we've gone to see Stewart's old flatmate."

"That line might serve you better," said Sinclair coldly.

"Don't worry about that, Sir Noah," said Pidgeon. "She doesn't exist. We just made her up to throw our super off. We'll just go back long-faced and say that we couldn't find her."

Sinclair found this rather funny. "Excellent," he said, laughing.

"Splendid," agreed Pidgeon. Splendid? thought Smudge. He was embarrassed. The lie had been his. He didn't like lying to Hartley—Smudge thought of himself as the type of man that always told the truth.

"So," said Sir Noah, "tell me what you have."

Smudge took two slim folders from his briefcase. "There's not a great deal here, I'm afraid."

For an hour Sinclair perused the documents. The photographs of the two victims he pronounced extraordinarily similar to those murdered in 1888.

"Mad, isn't he?" Sinclair remarked.

"There's a psychological profile there also," said Smudge.

Sinclair looked it over. "He sounds like most of the fellows of All Souls." He smiled.

Huddleston and Pidgeon knew it was a joke and they laughed dutifully.

"You don't really have much, do you?"

"No, sir," said Smudge.

"Grasping at straws, aren't you, by coming up here?"

"I'm afraid so, sir."

Pidgeon was bored. Sinclair couldn't do a damn thing for them, that much was obvious. It was just another wasted day, but a day that brought them a little closer to dropping the whole damn thing. Amen, said Pidgeon to himself.

Margaret opened the door and looked at the company for a second or two. "Lunch," she announced.

The meal, a surprisingly simple affair, was served not in a baronial dining hall, as Pidgeon and Huddleston might have expected, but in an orangery filled with flowers. It was a structure made of glass over a white iron framework, and its steep-pitched roof made it resemble a small iceberg whose stately progress over the Oxfordshire countryside had been interrupted by the Sinclair home against which it had come to rest.

It was a peculiar setting: a perfectly laid table in the midst of tropical plants, beyond which the diners could see a broad swatch of lawn, frozen and gray-brown in the liquid winter sun. Cutlery, knives and forks weighing about a pound each, enclosed each place setting like instruments in an operating room.

"Lovely," said Smudge.

Soup was served from a tureen on a serving cart by a man in a black jacket. A spirit lamp gently warmed the tureen.

Pidgeon, his heart leaping, instantly recognized the soup, the voice of Thérèse, the au pair girl, coming to him as if in a film flashback. Huddleston waited to see which spoon his hosts used before beginning his soup. He silently marveled at the manner in which Sir Noah and Lady Margaret acted in tandem with their servant: neither acknowledged his presence, but both availed themselves of his services completely.

"What kind of soup is this, darling?" asked Sir Noah, eyeing the pale-green liquid suspiciously.

Margaret hesitated a second and in that moment Pidgeon took command. "It's celeriac, isn't it?" he said, realizing that the chance to shine in gastronomic matters would probably never come his way again.

Margaret smiled a slight, superior smile—an expression he would come to know well. "A gourmet at Scotland Yard?"

"I take an interest in food," said Pidgeon, hoping that the conversation wouldn't go much further.

"The French have a name for this," she said. "I *can't* remember what it is." It was obviously a test question.

"*Céleri-rave,*" said Pidgeon, as if giving evidence in court. He could hear Thérèse complaining that you couldn't get *céleri-rave* in the supermarket in the Pimlico Road.

"Tell me, Inspector Pidgeon," Margaret continued, "do you prepare gourmet dinners for your colleagues in the CID?"

"I'm a detective sergeant, Lady Margaret," said Pidgeon, "and most of my colleagues prefer to eat in Wimpy bars."

"Inspector Huddleston, is that true?"

"Well," said Huddleston, wiping his mouth, "most of the lads don't know much about this sort of thing. I myself prefer to think that if it hasn't got a potato in it, it isn't really a meal. If you understand me."

Huddleston was trying to sound like homey old Smudge, dispensing good-natured, lower-middle-class wisdom. Pidgeon thought he sounded pretty stupid.

"Oh," said Lady Margaret, waving away her plate. She whispered to her server.

Smudge felt rather uncomfortable and silence fell on the table for a moment or two.

"These gentlemen are onto a marvelous case, Margaret. They've kindly asked me to assist them."

"Noah always wanted to be a policeman," said Margaret. "He's mad about murder."

"It's always surprising to me how many people are," said Pidgeon.

"History can be viewed in terms of murder," said Sir Noah. "Things would be very different now if a number of prominent people hadn't been murdered at the right time."

The server brought in a platter bearing a rack of lamb presented like a tent for Sir Noah's inspection.

"Lovely," he said. The man withdrew to carve.

Sinclair began explaining to Huddleston how history would have been different if the Duke of Clarence had not been murdered in 1478.

Plates were laid before each diner, two ribs of lamb and some braised endive. Resting alone on Smudge's plate, like a boulder, was a boiled potato, hurriedly prepared by Lady Margaret's cook. Smudge saw it and pulled his chin down into his chest in humiliation. Sir Noah looked at his meat for a second, not noticing Smudge's discomfort, and went on talking.

"Of course, one asks oneself, was not the execution of Sir Thomas More murder, or that of Charles I? Regicide, despite all the fine words about destroying tyrants, is just plain old murder. . . ."

Pidgeon noticed the potato on Smudge's plate and Margaret knew he had. He had had about enough.

"That was a rotten thing to do," he said quietly to her.

"I don't know what you mean," she said, looking not at all puzzled but haughty and beautiful. "Do you get up to Oxford often?" she asked blandly, to change the subject.

"No," said Pidgeon, "do you get to London?"

"Frequently. It gets a bit dull here."

"I can imagine," said Pidgeon.

"Can you? Where do you live in London?"

"Chelsea," said Pidgeon, with a touch of pride. She probably expected him to say Lambeth North.

"A gourmet police officer with a fashionable address," she said in wonder, leaving aside her lamb and lighting a cigarette. "I shouldn't imagine you'd be able to afford it on your salary." "I take bribes," said Pidgeon.

"Eh?" said Smudge. "What did you say?"

"It was a joke, Smudge," said Pidgeon.

"Smudge," said Sir Noah. "I like that. Is that what they call you down at the Yard, Inspector? Smudge Huddleston?"

"Well, sometimes, Sir Noah," said Smudge. "But my real name is Samuel."

"Prefer Smudge," said Sir Noah. "Much better."

As the Bentley carried Huddleston and Pidgeon away from the Sinclair home, Pidgeon said sarcastically, "I hope you're satisfied now. You've met a couple of aristocrats, had a slap-up meal, and a day away from the office. They're going to be dropping this case...."

"Sir Noah was a gent," said Huddleston, "and I've agreed to keep him informed. It was the least I could do, him being so kind."

Pidgeon took this news in silence. "She wasn't so bad either," said Pidgeon. "Not bad-looking, I mean."

"She was a bitch," said Smudge, with unexpected vehemence.

Listening to them, the chauffeur smiled to himself. They always said that about Lady Margaret.

CHAPTER EIGHT

At first Leary was afraid they were going to kill him. Jones had roused him that morning before sunrise, as he always did, and stood over him like his mother while he washed. Jones was a maniac for cleanliness, always picking at his nails or getting up abruptly to wash his hands, and he demanded a similar standard of hygiene in his charge.

Flynn was nowhere to be seen as they breakfasted in the kitchen of the farmhouse. The half-light of the gray winter morning made the chill in the room almost tangible. Jones, as usual, said nothing, and Leary, still numb with sleep, didn't mind. He drank his tea and watched Jones do the washing-up.

"Dress warm," said Jones, "we're going out."

"Bloody cold out. Where's Flynn?"

"Shut up," was all Jones would say.

A sharp wind was shipping across the moorland, freezing their ears and faces and making their eyes stream with tears. They followed a rough path through the crunchy, frozen bracken heading into the hills that lay low and sullen in the distance.

"Where're we going?" shouted Leary into the wind.

"Never you mind," Jones shouted back.

Leary felt his stomach lurch. It was then he first thought that Jones was going to kill him. He fought the panic as best he could, although he realized that Jones could do what he liked with him and no one would ever know.

They were walking in single file, Leary in front, Jones behind. Leary stopped shivering.

"Come on," said Jones, "get a move on."

Leary started moving again, stumbling a little.

"What's got into you?" demanded Jones at the top of his voice. Leary didn't answer. The path rose into the rocky hills, the landscape becoming grayer and meaner as they ascended. Jones pushed ahead.

"Follow me," he said.

Leary fell in behind him, followed Jones around some large boulders, saw the cave, and knew that he was a dead man. Jones entered the cave easily and unconcernedly, as if he were entering a pub. Leary stood outside staring into the gloom.

"Come on, Leary."

Leary turned and ran madly for the path to the low ground.

"Christ," said Jones, scrabbling out of the cave and pounding down the hillside after him. Leary tripped as Jones tackled him. Both men landed heavily, Jones on top of Leary on the loose rock of the hillside. Jones prayed that Leary hadn't broken anything.

"What the hell's gotten into you?"

Leary gasped for breath. "I know what you're planning to do to me."

"What are you talking about?"

"You're bringing me up here to do me in. The job's off, isn't it? Flynn disappears and you bring me up here to get rid of the evidence."

"You've gone round the bleeding bend, you have."

"Come on," said Leary, "I know you."

"I'm not going to do you in, Leary. You're too bloody valuable." He hated to have to praise his rather distasteful charge, but it had to be done.

"What did we come up here for?" Leary was a little calmer now.

"Training," said Jones.

"Training? Come on. . . ."

"Follow me, I'll show you."

As if he were leading a skittish horse through a gate, Jones coaxed Leary back into the cave. The wet gloom within was pierced by light entering through a fairly wide hole in the cave's roof.

"There," said Jones, pointing up the shaft. It ran straight through to the top of the hill, a good hundred and twenty feet. Staring up, Leary could see the sky. Set in the side of the shaft were large metal rungs about two feet apart. They ran to the top of the chimney, a shining silver ladder.

"What's that?" asked Leary.

"I told you," said Jones, "it's part of your training."

"Who put those things there?"

"We did."

"What for?"

"So you can learn to climb them."

"Climb them?" Leary looked up the shaft again.

"You've got to learn to climb them very quickly."

"What for?"

"Training," said Jones.

As Flynn entered the Dorchester Hotel on Park Lane, he looked like just another one of the hundreds of prosperous businessmen who would sweep through those revolving doors that day. Under an expensive-looking mohair overcoat he wore a dark suit and carried a briefcase made of a deep red leather. He thought he looked rather smart.

He took in the opulent lobby in a glance, spotted the lone hotel security man leafing through *The Financial Times*, and made directly for the number 4 elevator.

Security men and the services they provided constantly amazed him. They spent fortunes on hardware, they worked out complicated strategies for every conceivable situation, and yet they could be awfully sloppy, careless, stupid. Dignitaries had stayed at the Dorchester before, and in all cases the number 4 elevator was isolated for their exclusive use. Predictability was a security corps' greatest blunder.

He was lucky the first time—the elevator was empty. He pressed the button for the ninth floor, and as the door closed, he put his briefcase on the floor. He reached up to unscrew the two lug bolts that held the trap in the roof of the elevator shut. He pushed the hatch open without a problem. Flynn attached a piece of string to the handle of his case, jumped up, grabbed the lip of the trap, and swung himself up through the narrow opening to the roof of the car. He pulled his briefcase up after him and replaced the hatch. It was dark and dirty in the shaft, but Flynn felt quite comfortable knowing that he had all the time in the world. He watched with interest as the other three elevators in the shaft worked their way up and down, stopping at floors to pick up or discharge passengers.

Flynn's lift stopped at the ninth floor, then backed down to the eighth, where a couple got on. He could not see them very well through the fan housing, but he could hear their conversation perfectly.

"What would you like for lunch?"

"Oysters."

They didn't speak again. The lift stopped at six and again at four to pick up more passengers. Those who got on at four exchanged a sentence or two in French, in which Flynn, who had a fine ear for that sort of thing, was able to detect traces of a Lebanese accent.

He got down to work as the elevator emptied on the ground floor. From his briefcase he took a pocket torch and shone it over the roof of the car.

As the lift began a new trip upward, empty again, he found what he was looking for. A control board like the one inside the car lay to the left of the fan. Stamped on the metal scratchplate were the words FOR FIRE BRIGADE USE ONLY. Next to the message, flush with the metal of the board, was a keyhole.

A group of six or seven American men got into the lift on

five, going down. Flynn could feel the weight of them pull on the cable that stretched to the housing in the roof.

"Leyland will have to cover its losses this year," one of the men was saying, "if they plan on making a dent in the costs of retooling for the model changes next year."

"They'll never do it," said another.

"Good thing for us," said a third, and they all laughed and got off.

Flynn took an electric drill the size of a pocket shaver from his briefcase and fitted it with a drill bit just a hair thicker than a hypodermic needle.

The lift was now at lobby level. To Flynn's left he could hear the doors of the 2 and 3 elevators closing. He nodded to himself. The regulating system was holding the first and fourth elevators for a minute or two, as there wasn't enough business to occupy all four cars.

It also forced Flynn to wait until the lift started moving again, and he preferred that it be empty. The drill was quiet and he knew if worse came to worst he would be able to run it without attracting too much attention. But why risk it? He had plenty of time. He even considered having a cigarette, but there was too much grease and oil about.

The lift door swept shut, its stagger-time completed. It was empty, too.

"My lucky day," said Flynn, half aloud.

He slid a blank, unnotched Yale key into the control-panel lock. It did not turn, of course, but it did push all the tumblers up into the roof of the lock's cylinder. He placed the point of the drill bit just above the keyhole and pulled the trigger.

The drill whined and bit into the metal, skewering the five tumblers within the cylinder and breaking each at its midpoint. Flynn pulled the bit from the hole, broke down the drill, and stowed it neatly in his briefcase. Slowly, he removed the dummy key, hearing each tumbler fall into place. He dabbed a bit of grease from the main cable onto the hole, hiding any evidence of his tampering. It probably wasn't necessary, but you couldn't be too careful.

From the outside, the lock looked normal enough, untouched and secure. Flynn knew, however, that the whole mechanism was useless, locking nothing at all. Any blank key inserted into the roof lock would turn over control of the elevator to the panel on the roof. Flynn's deft work with the drill had eliminated the hours of tedious "tracing" that would have been necessary to get a molding from which a duplicate key could be made. The best feature of Flynn's lock tampering was that it was almost unnoticeable—if the real key was put in the lock, the whole mechanism would operate as it was meant to, arousing no suspicion.

"Now let's see if the bugger works," Flynn whispered to himself.

Two women got into the elevator.

"What floor, Sylvia?" said one.

"Eight."

Flynn turned the key in his board and pressed the button for nine.

Sylvia, watching the floor numbers light up above the door of the elevator, said in an annoyed tone, "It's going past, Margot."

"Damn," said Margot, pressing eight again.

Flynn took the lift down, from nine to eight, and let the two fuming women off.

"I shall complain," he heard Margot say.

He turned the key to the stop position and, for a moment, stopped the elevator between floors. Perfect.

He changed the system back to normal, lowered himself back into the car, and left the Dorchester through the lobby. No one noticed the grease stains on his shoes or on the elbow of his overcoat. The whole operation had taken less than thirty minutes.

Forty minutes after Flynn left the Dorchester, a representative of the Diplomatic Protection Group of the Metropolitan Police and a member of the United States Embassy Security

Service met with the hotel manager. The final security arrangements for Ambassador Coughlin's stay were discussed and agreed upon.

The hotel put the rooms on either side of the Coughlins' suite at the disposal of the embassy. An operations room would be put aside for the DPG near the lobby. Records of all the employees on duty in the residential part of the hotel were handed over for routine security clearance.

"The DPG is responsible for the ambassador's well-being in the lobby and in the rest of London," explained the man from the DPG.

"And we protect him when he's in his room," said the man from embassy security.

"We shall be isolating the number 4 elevator for Mr. Coughlin's use during his stay," said the manager. "That way, we'll be sure that the ambassador will not be in any danger."

"Good," said DPG.

"Much more secure," said embassy security.

As the two men left the hotel in search of a late lunch, the DPG man asked, "Why are they redecorating the ambassadorial residence now? Why not wait till they go to Washington? Save us all this fuss?"

"Beats the hell out of me," said the man from embassy security.

George VII, King of England by the Grace of God, lay in bed fully clothed. In the dark, on the floor next to his bed, he could make out an old pair of shoes, his oldest, the leather soles and uppers softened by years of wear. He had hidden them from his valet for fear that he would throw them away, since without those shoes George couldn't leave the palace without being detected. They were the only shoes that wouldn't give away that His Royal Highness was sneaking out, bent on mischief.

Never having had a great deal of it, George valued his privacy. The overriding element in his upbringing had been the abstract thing called his Duty. It made him conscious of his position and determined to do well by his subjects, but there were times when, like everybody else, he had to look out for himself.

He got out of bed and quietly slipped on the shoes. He took his notecase out of his jacket and counted the little cash that lay there. £26. Getting hold of cash was a very difficult operation—he couldn't just cash a check like everybody else, of course—and as he had no legitimate use for it, he couldn't ask someone to get him substantial amounts. He had to hoard what came his way until he had saved up a decent sum.

George put on a dark-blue overcoat and a shabby tweed hat, whose brim reached his ears, opened the door of his bedroom, and made his way across the study to the door that separated his suite from the rest of the palace.

Hunched by the door—dwarfed by it; it was twelve feet high—he studied the luminous dial of his wristwatch and waited.

A minute or two later the first of the palace clocks began chiming two, followed a few seconds later by another, and then another. Under the cover of the bells, George opened the door and walked quickly and silently down the corridor. He paused again at a service staircase in the south wing and, as the bells of Westminster Cathedral began to chime, made his way downstairs.

He had reached the point at which he could not back out. He was deep in the service wing of the building, following a corridor that led through a maze of laundries, storage rooms, and workshops. He was heading for the state apartments and the gardens beyond.

Three floors above him, Geoffrey Stanhope lay wide-awake in bed. Fear and worry lay deep in the pit of his stomach. He had no doubt that it was George who had so carefully made his way past his room; it had not been the first time he had heard the almost imperceptible sounds that suggested that Britain's King was taking an irregular tour of his demesne.

George was in the garden, facing the easiest part of his journey, although between him and the small gate at the northern

95

point of the palace grounds lay acres of well-lit garden that were patrolled at regular intervals by the palace division of the Special Branch.

He stood in the shadows by the lawn's edge and waited for a minute or two. A sharp, cold wind whipped off the ornamental lake, numbing his cheeks. From the eastern end of the grounds, far off, came the sounds of a dog whining and the jingling of its collar. George allowed himself to relax a bit. Constable Poole was on time.

George could see him quite distinctly, crossing the lawn, dragging his footsteps a bit to keep the dog in check. The dog, an Alsatian bitch named Wilma, led Poole directly to George.

"Good evening, sir," said Poole. "Perishin' cold."

"Yes," agreed George. He glanced round him nervously. "You are sure none of the rest of the squad is about?"

"There's one of the chaps doing the rounds by the Mews, sir. But he won't disturb us. I'm doing the half-two patrol as usual. . . . Me and Wilma." He rubbed the dog's ears affectionately.

"Well," said George, "we'd better be off. . . ."

"Right, sir," said Poole, leading the way down the western edge, through the trees and shrubbery.

It had taken a bit of doing to recruit Poole. During the late summer and early autumn George had taken to smoking a cigar in the garden late at night before retiring. In doing so he had met and befriended Constable Poole, one of the members of the Palace Division of the Special Branch. Gradually, George had felt confident enough of Poole's sense of discretion to confide in him: he explained that he needed a means of slipping out of the palace. Poole—who said he had been young himself once—had agreed to help. At half past two every night, he would leave the police squad room and go on patrol. If George was waiting for him, Wilma led the policeman there. Poole then escorted George to the tiny gate in the west wall and let him out. At four-thirty Poole would be waiting to let him back in. Poole had not asked for payment and had never inquired where George went.

For George, the hardest part of his escape was opening the

door in the wall and stepping out into the glare of the street lamps lining Grosvenor Place. He tried to act as if it were the most natural thing in the world.

"You'll be all right, sir?" asked Poole.

"Yes, quite all right."

A single motorist bombed by in a Vauxhall, taking no notice of George. He pulled his hat farther down onto his head. He had been sweating since he left his room, and only now, outside the palace walls, did his damp skin catch the wind and cool.

He crossed the street using the pedestrian subway at Hyde Park Corner, looking over his shoulder as the brick wall enclosing the palace disappeared behind him.

George crossed Grosvenor Crescent, walked west toward Knightsbridge, and felt, as he always did on these nights, curiously elated. London slept around him, unaware of his presence. He felt like singing, or at least humming to himself, but didn't.

CHAPTER NINE

Jason's mummy and Jason's daddy were having a fight. Jason, who was six, held himself slightly aloof.

The three of them were walking along the Chelsea Embankment, approaching the Albert Bridge. Jason's dog, Smartie, named for a popular sweet, trotted ahead of the family, pausing to inspect bits of pavement that struck him as interesting. Jason stared out over the river, half listening as his mother complained that his father spent too much money, her money, for drinking and carrying on. Jason's father said that just because her family was filthy rich he wasn't going to kowtow.

"What's kowtow?" asked Jason.

"Oh, Christ," said his mother.

To the motorist speeding by on the embankment road they looked like a perfect family group. The two parents deep in conversation on their morning stroll, their son and heir walking along next to them, staring through the railings lining the walk at the few feet of grass and the tugs and the garbage on the river beyond.

Jason gradually lost all interest in his parents' wrangle—it wasn't anything new to him. He could see the gray plains of

Battersea Park across the river, dominated by the citadel of the power station.

"Honestly, Raymond, we cannot go on like this."

"I know, Madeline, I know."

As they neared the Albert Bridge, the bushes between Jason and the river got thicker, robbing him of most of his view. He studied the refuse that had accumulated beneath the rather bedraggled foliage. There were old newspapers and empty lager tins and ice-cream wrappers. Shredded magazines, sodden by the rain, lay flat and pulpy on the ground like mold.

Jason stopped, peering seriously and intently through the bars, much in the same manner as he did in the zoo when he encountered a particularly hideous animal. There was something there, something wet and dead and nasty, and Jason, staring, felt fear curling through his body.

His parents walked on, Jason's father explaining that Jason's mother was turning into a first-class bitch. Jason looked up from the bars and stared at his parents' backs. He snuffled, and a tear dripped down his face as he turned to look back between the bars once again.

"Jason, come on!" shouted his mother.

Jason looked at her.

"Jason!"

"Daddy!" Jason wailed.

"What's the matter with him?" he asked her.

"He wants you to go and get him. Not me, of course. . . ."

Jason's father walked back toward his son. "What's the matter, sausage?" he asked, kneeling down next to him.

Jason pointed through the bars. Raymond was unable, at first, to identify the raw bundle that was the cause of Jason's disquiet. Then it fit.

"God!" He grabbed Jason and buried the child's face in his shoulder. "Don't look."

"Raymond, what the hell is going on?"

"A body," said Raymond. "Jesus!"

The coroner would later establish that the woman had died by strangulation and had been eviscerated in situ, between the hours of 3:00 and 4:00 a.m.

"I'm getting a bit sick of this," said Pidgeon, as the remains of "White female, 17–25 years, file C-6221" were slid back into the mortuary drawer. He glanced around the white-tiled room, one wall lined with the green metal cabinets that contained the remains of Londoners who had come to violent or suspicious ends.

"Don't blame you," said the attendant, "she's a mess."

"Don't take this the wrong way, Tony," said Smudge, "but those marks on her face. . ."

"What about them?" said Pidgeon irritably. The room was cold and clammy. There was an odd and disturbing smell in the air.

Huddleston slowly pulled the drawer back open and raised the sheet. The woman's mouth was slack and puffy, her eyes closed. It was impossible to say if she had ever been pretty. Dried blood had collected on her cheekbones.

"You see—there," said Smudge, pointing at, but not touching, the woman's lower eyelids. "These cuts under her eyes."

"Yeah."

"Catherine Eddowes had the same thing."

"Catherine who?" He said impatiently. He was anxious to leave.

"Catherine Eddowes, Ripper victim number 3. September 30, 1888."

Pidgeon sighed. "Give over, Smudgie."

WHO'S NEXT? inquired the *Sun.*
TERROR! announced the *Mirror.*

On ITV news a prostitute, her face obscured, said, " 'E's going to have to do an M.P.'s wife before the police take any notice."

100

Hansard, the parliamentary reporter, recorded the following exchange:

> Mr. GREENE (Lab., Putney): I would like to ask the Home Secretary what is being done to protect the single women of London from vicious attacks on their person.
> MR. BARNETT (Home Sec.): The honourable member is aware that the victims are known prostitutes?
> MR. GREENE: Known to whom, sir? (Laughter from Opposition back benches.)

"And what have you done to earn your wages?" asked Alf Hartley of Huddleston and Pidgeon. He leaned back in his swivel chair, planted his feet on top of the desk, and looked expectant.

They looked at each other. "We're talking to the foot patrols operating in the neighborhood, also the Q and E cars . . ." said Huddleston uncertainly, like a schoolboy asked to conjugate an irregular Latin verb.

"And we're making inquiries about the woman's identity . . ." said Pidgeon lamely.

"Oh, very nice," said Hartley sarcastically. "Making inquiries."

"Chelsea isn't a neighborhood for toms, so we're checking with the girls in Paddington and Soho, the lower-class prostitutes, to see if they've noticed anyone missing. How she got to the Chelsea Embankment is anyone's guess."

"You guess," said Hartley, slipping a cigarette into his mouth and lighting it, "and then I'll give you your reward."

"He picked her up—" said Huddleston, looking at the ceiling.

"—and said he fancied a roll in the bushes?" finished Pidgeon hesitantly.

"Here," said Hartley, slinging an envelope across the desk. "You don't deserve it, but here it is."

"What is it?" said Pidgeon.

"Open it outside." Hartley returned to his paperwork.

Pidgeon tore open the envelope, Huddleston crowding in at his side. Inside was a typewritten sheet wrapped around a small, clear-plastic envelope, which contained a triangular piece of metal broken raggedly along one edge.

Pidgeon skimmed the letter, then smiled triumphantly. "We've got him, Smudge."

Huddleston snatched the piece of paper from Pidgeon's hand:

> *The enclosed piece of metal (carbon steel, 2cm by 8cm by 4cm, 0.2mm thickness) was found during the autopsy on case file C-6221. A secondary but forceful thrust, probably intended for the victims's vulva, missed its mark, striking instead the left femur close to its conjunction with the pelvic girdle. The force of the blow and the strength of the femur at that point resulted in the enclosed chip of metal, the tip of the murder weapon, breaking off from the blade of the knife.*
>
> *Initial forensic reports indicate that the alloy and the configuration of the blade correspond to a Nepalese weapon, the kukri, carried by the Gurkha divisions of the British Army as recently as 1971.*

"We've got him now," said Pidgeon.

Huddleston smiled. "You just might be right at that."

The mail had been cleared away and in its place had come hundreds of dun-colored dossiers, files culled from army records of the former members of the ten Gurkha rifle regiments now living in London.

Pidgeon skimmed each quickly, sorting them into piles much as he had done with the Cuckoo post. Of the men who had served in the Rifles—they were dealing with officers exclusively—there did not yet seem to be a single candidate for what the office was calling the "Mad Gurkha."

Robert Hoophouse, DSO, retired service 1947. Rank: brevet-major. Died 1956.

Walter Waring, retired service 1949. Rank: captain. Director, Dar-Es-Salaam Tea Company. Present address: The Willows, Croydon.

"They're all so bloody respectable," said Pidgeon under his breath.

Anthony Ackerly, retired service 1956. Rank: lieutenant. Died 1964. (Boating accident, Henley on Thames.)

"Find anything good?" asked Huddleston, who approached Pidgeon's desk with a flat, brown paper parcel and an air of Look-what-I've-got. He laid the package on the desk.

"What's that?"

"Open it."

Pidgeon stripped away the paper. Inside was a sheath knife, fully a foot long, pinched in the middle to give it a peculiar dog-leg shape. Pidgeon eased it from its case.

"God," he said, "that's nasty."

"Just the ticket for doing a number of unpleasant deeds," said Smudge.

"Blimey, Tony," said Lennie Harris from the next desk, "don't lose your temper."

Pidgeon waved the weighty blade at him. "You're the first, Harris."

"Is it true you can throw one of those things and it'll come back to you like a boomerang?" asked Harris.

"Ask Smudge. He's been doing a lot of reading on the subject. He's a great one for reading, is Smudge."

"You can't throw one of these. Too heavy."

"What's this?" said Pidgeon, pointing to a half-moon notch cut in the blade at the point where the handle met the blade.

"No one really knows. It's thought to be a symbol for the female genitalia," Smudge said primly.

"That would fit," said Pidgeon.

"Did you know any Gurkhas when you were in the service, Tony?"asked Harris.

"No. They were all in Hong Kong. Signals mostly, I think."

"I knew some," said Hartley, coming out of his office and leaning on the doorframe. "Military Police in Singapore, after the war. Funny buggers."

"They as ferocious as their reputation?" asked Harris.

"I never noticed. 'Course, I never saw them in combat. They kept to themselves mostly. They aren't much over five feet, most of them. They had British officers, I think."

"Lots of British officers," said Pidgeon, pointing at the files. "They loved the Scottish regiments. Don't know why."

"It's safe to assume that we're not looking for a little Nepalese blighter, then," said Pidgeon.

"Well," said Hartley, "I'm not exactly sure what a Nepalese accent sounds like, but I'll bet you that wasn't one on our recording."

"So we're stuck with these." He gestured toward the folders.

"Piece of cake," said Hartley, turning toward his office.

"There's just one thing," said Huddleston.

"What's that?"

"Well, you don't have to be a Gurkha to own a kukri. I bought this one at a military antiques shop in Thayer Street. And take a look at how thick this blade is. I find it hard to believe that it broke off when it struck Phoebe's thigh." They had not yet identified the dead woman. Someone had started calling her Phoebe and the name had stuck.

"I think it's unlikely that she put it there herself, don't you, Smudgie?"

"Still . . ."

"Check the Gurkhas first," Hartley instructed. "Ask them to show you their kukris . . ."

"Oooh, you saucy boy," said Harris.

"Shut up, Lennie. These blokes must have kept theirs as souvenirs. If one has a broken point, you've got your man."

"Nobody is going to be that stupid," said Pidgeon.

"People do funny things," said Hartley.

The elimination of suspects is, perhaps, the most tedious part of police work. Officers must ask the same questions again and again of dozens of usually mystified, always wary, sometimes hostile people. Smudge and Pidgeon were assigned six plainclothes constables to assist them. They roamed the Home

Counties and talked to Gurkha hands and looked at their war souvenirs.

Interviews became as predictable as oft-rehearsed scenes from a play. The cast was always the same—two policemen and a third, older man, usually of military bearing—and so was the script.

"Did you take any souvenirs with you from the army, sir?"

"Yes" was the usual answer to that. Was that not allowed?

"Did you happen to take a kukri, sir?"

Officers didn't carry kukris as part of their kit, but yes, many of the officers had taken one of these peculiarly Gurkha weapons with them.

"May we see it, sir?"

"Good Lord" was the usual reply. Few of them were ever quite sure where it was. "After all these years, you can imagine . . ."

None had a broken point.

"Does anyone else have access to this weapon, sir?"

"The wife" was the usual answer. In a few cases, the wife and the servants.

The most dangerous type the investigators were likely to encounter were the military bores.

"Gurkhas? Yes, I was with the Ninth. Damn fine little soldiers—glad they were on our side, I can tell you. At Monte Cassino, I remember, hell of a scrap, took us days, you know. Brigade was on our flank, here, you see, and one afternoon my CO says take a few chaps and cut along to Brigade HQ. . . ."

"Kukri? Yes, with the Chindits in Burma. I saw our lads cut the enemy up with those devilish things. Better than bayonets in tight quarters. I remember once, there was a Jap patrol . . ."

There were those who no longer had their weapon: "Sold it, 'bout ten years back. To a collector. He gave me a fair price for it, but they are worth a damn sight more now, I'll be bound. . . ."

And those who "Presented it to the War Museum, in Lambeth. Someplace, I've got a note from them thanking me."

It was dull, tiring, fruitless work. Each day, Huddleston, Pidgeon, and their six complaining assistants set out on their rounds loaded up with more names. Smudge gave out the assignments.

"Lots of these blokes are dead," he said, going through the files.

"Not enough of them," said Pidgeon, lowering his chin into his hands.

"Well, here's one you don't have to worry about," said Huddleston, staring at a file.

"Who is it?"

"Take a look."

Pidgeon took the folder and glanced at it. "Christ, Colonel-in-Chief, Twelfth Gurkha Rifles. These blokes in army records are thorough." He smiled. "Fancy a trip up to the palace, Smudgie?"

"I don't think we need bother His Majesty, do you?" said Smudge seriously.

"Bring him in for questioning, I say," said Harris. "Work him over proper."

Geoffrey Stanhope got down from the first-class compartment at the Oxford station and stretched. The station was as familiar to him as his own bedroom; he had come and gone through it dozens of times when he had been up at Balliol.

"Captain Stanhope?"

"Glover," said Stanhope. "I'm glad to see you. How's Sir Noah?"

"Fit, sir."

"I expect nothing less of him."

"The car, sir," said Glover, gesturing toward the main door of the station.

Stanhope and Glover did not speak during the ride to the house. For Stanhope, the road to Meetcham was lined with a thousand undergraduate memories.

He had once been a member of the Sinclair Set, a throwback to the days of Bowra, Hogarth, and Jowett, when the brightest undergraduates had gathered around a brilliant don who guided them, teased them, and molded their futures. In the hothouse atmosphere of Oxford, Sinclair had been the intellectual mentor of young men who had gone on to become financiers, politicians, writers, civil servants—at that moment, four Sinclair protégés were cabinet ministers. None had forgotten their patron.

It was a well-known fact in certain circles that Noah Sinclair was the center of a very powerful network. Through the people he had adopted, educated, and launched, Sinclair was able to exert subtle but powerful influences in almost any area of public policy that interested him. Sinclair was the person to see if one wanted a pet project adopted, or a career made or ruined.

Stanhope was part of a younger crop. His contemporaries were still only halfway up the ladder of power, but each knew—and Sinclair knew—that they would get there in the end, because Sir Noah ordained it.

Margaret met him at the door.

"Geoffrey, still so dashingly boyish," she said, kissing him lightly on the cheek. "How's HRH the King?"

"Opening the last word in abattoirs in Bristol. I managed to get out of it," he said, smiling. Margaret had been part of the set when Stanhope had been up. She had bludgeoned her way into Oxford, fresh from her first marriage, and then forced her way into the circle around Sinclair. Society was surprised but not upset when she married him; she fit in well. Rumor had it that she took her own, specialized interest in Sinclair's protégés.

"Who's escorting the King?"

"His private secretary."

"Randolph must be angry. He hates to leave London."

"He's livid," said Stanhope, and they both laughed.

"Going back tonight?"

"Yes, on the 4:45."

"Good. I'm going in; we can ride together. There's some party in Belgravia—Noah insists that I go. He's in his lair, by the way."

"I know the route."

Stanhope walked down the wide and ill-lit hallway to the door of Sinclair's study. He knocked and entered.

Sinclair greeted Stanhope warmly. "How's the palace?"

"Well, Noah, that's why I'm here."

"You seem rather put out, Geoffrey."

Stanhope bit his upper lip. "Things look rather peculiar."

"Peculiar?" said Sinclair. "Things look terrible. My Exchequer friends tell me that the whole damn government is coming unstuck for lack of money. The Intelligence boys at the Ministry of Defence say that South Africa is about to blow wide open. You know what that means, don't you?"

"Well, no, actually, But—"

"It means that if there's civil war there—and that's how things are shaping up—we'll have, among other things, white wave immigration here. That means more unemployment, more racial tension. I don't even want to think what this'll do to our business interests there. And the gold! It could play havoc with currencies worldwide. The whole thing could be terribly nasty."

"Terribly," agreed Stanhope. "Noah, I don't mean to add to your problems, but I'm rather worried about— Well, of course, it could be nothing."

Sinclair smiled and opened his arms wide. "Unburden yourself."

"Well, I'm sure you are following the new Ripper crimes. . . ."

"Of course. Fascinating."

"Well—" Stanhope took a deep breath. "I think George may have something to do with them."

Sinclair's laughter rocked the room. "Geoffrey, you need a holiday. See if you can borrow someone's house in Corfu."

Stanhope sat immobile, smiling thinly at Sinclair's amusement. "I know it sounds ridiculous. . . ."

"You know, of course, that the prime suspect in the original crimes was the heir to the throne."

"I had heard that. Everyone has at one time or another, but honestly, Noah, you know I wouldn't come to you with this if I didn't think it was worth your time."

"I'm sorry, Geoffrey. Tell me what you know."

Stanhope explained. George had left the palace three times

that he knew of in the last two months. Following each night out, a crime had been committed. In the case of the last two, the bodies had been discovered the next day.

"The police said that the corpse of the first girl wasn't found for three or four days. That would work back to the first night I noticed George leaving."

"Geoffrey," said Sinclair gravely, "don't you think it's rather unlikely that he'd commit a murder during coronation week?"

"I think the whole thing is bloody unlikely," said Geoffrey quietly. "I've known him for years and I've never suspected that anything was peculiar about him. . . ." Stanhope stressed "peculiar."

"Your having known him for years doesn't make a dent in the sense of isolation he must feel. . . . But let's look at the facts. Surely if he went wandering around someone would recognize him?"

"It's been cold. He'd be all bundled up. Besides, a prostitute is hardly expecting to be picked up by the King, is she? And even if she recognized him, she wouldn't have a great deal longer to live."

"Of course." Sinclair lit a cigar. "You know, I have some knowledge of this case. Inside knowledge."

Stanhope smiled. "Inevitably."

"I've just received a note from my friend Inspector Huddleston—he's leading the investigation, and rather hopeless at it, I'm afraid. He wrote that there has been rather a breakthrough in the case: a detail that hasn't been released to the press. It seems that a piece of the murder weapon has been found embedded in the thigh of the last victim. It's a piece of one of those Gurkha knives."

"A kukri?"

Sinclair laughed. "Forgive me, but I always find that word rather funny."

"You know," said Stanhope, "George must have one someplace. . . . One of the regiments made him honorary Colonel-in-Chief."

"Is it missing its tip?"

"Lord, I've no idea."

"Why don't you see if you can find out? Just for the sake of interest."

"Snoop?"

"Yes, why not?"

"Seems rather shabby, that's all."

"Tell me, you've never followed him out at night?"

"No."

"Or confronted him?"

"Noah, he is the King, after all."

"Yes. So he is," said Sinclair meditatively.

Each considered for a minute or two the consequences of George's actions.

"What if he is the murderer?" said Stanhope. "What a catastrophe it would be. It might be the end of the monarchy itself. . . ."

"First," said Sinclair matter-of-factly, "we must find out if he is the killer. And if he is—" He paused, measuring the weight of his words.

"Yes?"

"Close ranks, my boy. Protect our own."

It was eleven o'clock and Pidgeon was asleep in an armchair in front of the murmuring television set. On the coffee table in front of him lay the remains of his evening meal—a hamburger and peas with onions. A fairly deep swatch of tomato sauce was spread across the plate, the bottle standing open on the table. Next to that were bottles of HP and Worcestershire sauce, plus a bottle of A-1 that he hadn't used. It had not been a fancy meal. The Bisquit and an empty glass stood at his feet.

He woke up, aware that he was dreaming something, but before he could catch hold of it and remember it, the dream slipped away. Then he heard the telephone.

Not again, he thought.

He hoisted himself from the chair and dove across the bed to catch the phone.

"Pidgeon?" It was a woman's voice.

"Yes?" It was familiar.

"Maggie Sinclair."

"What a surprise!" And it was.

"Yes, I thought it might be." He could hear the smile in her voice, above the confusion of noises in the background.

"Where are you?"

"I'm at a party. In London. Nearby, in Lyall Street."

A sentence formed itself in Pidgeon's mind. Come round for a drink, it said, but came out: "How are you?"

"I'm all right. You?"

"Can't complain." Come round for a drink, he thought again.

"Well . . ." she said.

"Okay . . ." he said.

"Good-bye."

"Good-bye." And he hung up. "You stupid bastard," he said aloud, seeing her in his mind's eye hanging up and returning to the party as embarrassed and mystified as he was.

The phone rang again. "Why didn't you invite me over for a drink?" she asked.

"I was going to, but you hung up."

"You don't sound terribly keen," she said, as if they were old lovers.

"I am," Pidgeon protested.

"I'll be along."

"Twenty-eight, Sloane—"

"I know the address," she said.

After she hung up, Pidgeon held the receiver in his hand and looked at the ceiling. "Thank you, God."

Pidgeon gaped at the living room, wondering where to start. He scooped up his dinner plate, the fork, and the bottles, deftly imprinting stains on his shirt. He hurried into the kitchen and dropped everything into a large biscuit tin in which he usually stored bread.

Tearing his shirt open, he made for the bathroom, caught a glimpse of himself in the mirror—he looked tired—and quickly doused his face with cold water. He swept the toilet articles off

111

the edge of the sink and jammed them into the medicine chest. He picked up the copy of *Private Eye* (open to Auberon Waugh's diary, a feature he never read) that lay near the toilet. In his bedroom, he jammed the magazine and his dirty shirt under the bed. For the next few seconds he alternated between buttoning his clean shirt and smoothing down the rumpled bed. Then the door bell rang.

"This is a pleasant surprise," he said, opening the door.

"I was in the neighborhood."

"Come in."

She was dressed in a loose sheath of gray silk that fell in a razor-sharp line from her shoulders to the floor. In her hand, she carried a silver fox jacket that looked as if it were worth twice Pidgeon's yearly wages. He doubted he could have covered the cost of the platinum-and-diamond collar around her neck with his life pension.

"You're a bit overdressed," he said, smiling.

She stepped into the living room just a bit warily, as if she'd been invited into a cave.

"This is very nice," she said. Then she caught sight of *London's Underworld*. "You continue to astound me."

"A gift," he said. "I hate it."

"I'm afraid it doesn't exactly speak to me either."

"I'm afraid all I can offer you is some brandy."

"Perfect."

As he fetched the drinks, Pidgeon wondered quite suddenly what on earth he was going to say to this woman. They shared no points of reference, no friends in common; his complaints were unlikely to be hers—they couldn't even commiserate on how high prices and rents were. He realized how often he and the people he knew referred to money or rather the lack of it— "If I won the pools, the first thing I'd do . . ."—knowing full well that they'd always be pressed for cash. It was a world she didn't know or understand or probably even care about. As for taking her to bed—well, he might as well hope to win the Irish sweep.

"How was the Irish sweep?" he asked, and colored immediately.

"Good," she said, assuming it to be slang for "party." "Better than I expected."

"I trust we made a good impression on Sir Noah?"

"He tends to make impressions on others, actually." She sipped the brandy.

Pidgeon was about to say that Sir Noah didn't strike him as all that wonderful and decided not to.

"You'll forgive my asking," he said, "but why did you come here tonight?"

She laughed. "Because I find you attractive."

His heart leaped. "Fair enough," he said calmly. "Going back to Oxford tonight?"

"Heavens, no."

"And Sir Noah?"

"At home. I've done this before."

"Have you?"

"I'm not expected home till midday tomorrow."

Midday, thought Pidgeon. She was the kind of woman who said midday instead of noon or twelve o'clock. He put his glass down, acutely aware that he was about to make a pass at a woman richer, more sophisticated, and more socially advanced than himself, and married to a knight.

"So," he said, and kissed her.

Margaret stretched next to him, lifted her arms above her head, and yawned. He smiled and tried to remember exactly what her legs had felt like as they pinioned his a few moments before. Nice—good and strong, he decided.

"What time is it?" she asked.

"Twelve-fifteen."

"Phone," she demanded. "I must ring Noah."

"Why?"

"Because I always do." She lifted the receiver and dialed, sitting up on her legs in the middle of the bed. Pidgeon was glad to see that she did not coyly wrap the sheet around herself.

"Bates, it's Lady Margaret."

Her skin was still damp from their lovemaking and it shone

dully in the little light in the room. Her breasts lay shallow against her chest, not looking like tacked-on-afterthoughts, Pidgeon thought, as they did on some women. She brushed the hair from her eyes.

"Noah, darling. Yes, the party was fine." She was silent as Sinclair said something.

"Mildred and Freddie send their love."

Another pause.

"Yes, on the eleven-fifteen. Good night, lovey."

She lay back on the pillows and sighed.

Pidgeon regarded her for a moment. "Why are you married to him?"

"That's rather impertinent."

"Beg pardon, Lady Margaret."

She lit a cigarette. "If you'd known my first husband, you'd understand."

"First husband?"

"Yes. I made just the sort of first marriage I was expected to. A young rich man from an old rich family I met when I came out. A perfect match, everyone said. And they were right—we were a beautiful couple. Except . . ."

"Yes?"

"You want to know all the gory details?"

"Yes," he said. "Policemen love gory details."

"He was a bore. A bore. And rotten in bed. Used to buy magazines, you know, they all had names like *Squire* and *Stud.* Women with big knockers and spread legs. It was so pathetic. He went to New York on a business trip once and brought one back called *Wet Pussy. Wet Pussy,* I ask you."

Pidgeon wasn't sure what to say. Sinclair didn't look like much of a sexual bargain either.

"I took all I could," said Margaret evenly, "and then one night I walked out on him."

"What made you leave?"

Margaret laughed. "It was so embarrassing."

"What was?"

"One night, he got into bed, having read enough of *Wanker's Weekly* to want to try to fuck me—"

114

Pidgeon found the obscenities, so easily said, quite captivating.

"—doubtless in his mind pretending I was 'Breasty Betty: The Girl Who Never Says No,' page 56, and he was so excited he blacked out and fell off the bed."

"So?"

"He broke his nose. He lay there groaning and looking thoroughly ridiculous." Margaret exhaled. "Poor little man. Now, Noah, on the other hand, is charming, very rich, extremely powerful, learned . . . And sexually, I'm allowed to take care of myself."

"Oh," said Pidgeon, hollowly.

"Now, don't go getting all offended."

"No," said Pidgeon defensively. "Why should I?"

"Men do, sometimes."

"Do they?"

"Yes," she said. "They do."

"Oh."

"Listen," she said casually. "I heard some news that might interest you." Then she told him about Stanhope and the King's nights out.

"You're joking," he said.

"I am not," she said firmly.

"Come on . . ."

"Honestly," she protested.

"Why are you telling me—if your husband is so intent on seeing that nobody finds out?"

She wriggled in the bed and giggled. "I think it would be rather fun, putting the King on trial. Oliver Cromwell did it."

"You're having me on." He had half risen from the bed and was facing her.

"No, honestly."

"What do you think I am?" He ran his hand through his hair.

"Actually, I think you're rather sexy," she said, pulling him close.

"Wait," he said, trying to pull back.

"Why?" she asked, smiling.

She awoke while he was dressing.

"No need to get up yet," he said, smoothing her hair on the pillow.

"Morning, Pidgeon," she said.

"I've got to get to work," he said.

"To catch the King." She smiled sleepily.

"Don't talk about that," he said sternly. "Listen, there's coffee on the stove and the number of a taxi service next to the phone. The door locks behind you, so you can leave when you like."

"Hmm," she said.

He sat on the edge of the bed awkwardly.

"Come here, Pidgeon," She put her hands on his shoulders and looked at him more affectionately than he expected. "I'll call," she said, and kissed him.

When he left, she was asleep again. She awoke at ten, feeling pretty good but hungry. She made her way to the kitchen, thinking that she'd look rather odd trooping through London in evening dress on a Thursday midmorning.

In the biscuit bin she was puzzled to find a dirty plate, four bottles of sauce, and a fork.

CHAPTER
TEN

It was one of those rare mornings when almost all of the staff was in the squad room at once. Typewriters were being pounded at most desks, a few men were hunched over telephones. Smudge was typing one of Lennie Harris's reports, clicking his tongue whenever he came across a spelling error.

"Honestly, Lennie. Where did you learn to spell?"

"I never learnt, Smudge. I just have a natural flair for it."

Pidgeon came in and hung up his coat.

"Morning, Smudge, Lennie. Busy here this morning," he said, looking around him.

"Morning, Tony," said Smudge.

"Ah, Pidgeon of the Yard. Good morning," said Harris, doing a rather good upper-class accent.

Pidgeon slid into his seat and watched Smudge tapping away at the keyboard. "Doing this lazy bugger's work again, Smudge?"

"Only take a minute."

"Smudge was my batman in the army," said Harris. "First-rate little valet."

"Fancy going down to the caf for a cup of tea?"

Harris clasped his hands to his chest. "He asked me! Big, brawny, handsome Detective Sergeant Pidgeon noticed me. Arabella, I feel I shall faint."

"Not you, Lennie. Smudge."

"Denied again," said Harris in false melancholy.

"No thanks, Tony," said Smudge brightly. "I just had some."

"I think you better have another," said Pidgeon, pulling him up by the shoulders.

"Well, if you insist," said Huddleston, puzzled.

"Careful, Smudge, he'll break your heart," said Harris.

"You need a bloody holiday, Lennie," said Pidgeon, as he pushed Smudge toward the door.

In the canteen, Pidgeon sat Huddleston at a table and got tea for both of them.

"Well?" asked Smudge.

"Well," said Pidgeon, "I've got news." He gestured with his hands as if to erase his words. "I'm not sure what I've got. It could just be a joke. Or something. I'm not sure. . . ."

"Tony," said Smudge, amazed, "I have no idea what you're talking about."

Pidgeon took a deep breath. "Hang on to your hat, Smudgie." He leaned halfway across the table and began talking quickly in little more than a whisper.

"The King?" said Smudge, a little too loudly.

"Shut up, will you? I don't believe it either. But you yourself said that one of the old Ripper suspects was a bloody Royal. Maybe it's an hereditary trait."

"Tony," said Huddleston solemnly, "this conversation is treasonous."

"Oh, for Christ's sake."

Huddleston's eyes narrowed. "Where did you pick up this bit of nonsense?"

"Never you mind where. It's highly reliable, though."

"Who, Tony?" said Smudge sternly.

"Margaret Sinclair."

"Tony, she's playing you for a fool. You know what she's like."

"Why would she make up something like that?"

"To make an ass out of you."

"She's telling the truth. She overheard her husband talking about it with some bugger from the palace."

"Tony, you do realize what you're saying?"

"Of course, it sounds bloody unlikely. But him disappearing like that at the right time—it's quite a coincidence."

"Yes," Smudge admitted.

"So, we wait till Margaret Sinclair finds out about the murder weapon."

"Oh," said Smudge sarcastically. "She'll come running to tell us all about it, right?"

Pidgeon grinned. "She'll tell me, Smudgie."

"Lothario," said Huddleston, in genuine disapproval.

A king's wardrobe consists, among other things, of dozens of military uniforms. There are the ceremonial uniforms designating his overall rank in the British armed forces—Admiral of the Fleet, Air Marshal for the RAF—and others reflecting his association with special regiments—the Royal Regiment of Wales, Colonel in the Welsh Guards, Colonel-in-Chief of the Gordon Highlanders—each with its own version of mess dress, service dress, summer uniform, winter uniform. Added to these are the court ceremonials, the Windsor uniform, and the Garter dress, each to be worn with the proper decorations and orders.

The King's uniforms are kept in a separate room in the palace, and Geoffrey Stanhope had had until recently only the vaguest notion of where it was. He found out by asking a backstairs page. The uniforms were kept next to the room that housed the King's personal valet, Mr. Rhodes.

Luncheon is served in the upper servants' hall precisely at noon. As Mr. Rhodes entered the hall for lunch, Geoffrey Stanhope entered the uniforms room seven floors above him.

It was a narrow room, not much more than a large closet.

The dark wood cabinets were labeled neatly. The first one that caught his eye was Commander, Royal Navy, Mediterranean Squadron. To the left of that: Colonel, King's Royal Rifle Corps. And next to that: Colonel-in-Chief, Royal Parachute Regiment.

He worked down the room, reading the rest. Near the window he found Colonel-in-Chief, 12th King George V Own Gurkhas.

He swept the closet open. The jet black dress tunic and trousers hung there, and next to them the summer whites. They smelled faintly of mothballs. Beneath the tunics was a small chest of drawers. Stanhope opened the first and found, neatly folded, the black gloves of the uniform and the dark metal chains worn from the left shoulder across the breast belt. In the drawer beneath that, in a black leather case, was a kukri.

Stanhope wrapped his hand in a handkerchief and slowly pulled the blade an inch from the sheath. Under the stock of the blade was an inscription: "Presented to HRH the Prince of Wales, Colonel-in-Chief, 12th Gurkha Rifles." Geoffrey swept the blade from the scabbard and stared blankly at the broken tip.

"Sir Noah," said Smudge to Pidgeon, "cannot be called to the telephone. His man says that he's busy. He'll ring me back."

"Fat chance," said Pidgeon. "I don't think we'll be having too many more dealings with Sir Noah."

Smudge stuck his pipe in his mouth. "I want to know why he's withholding evidence."

"It's not evidence till we know about the knife."

"When'll we know?" asked Smudge, sucking on the stem.

"Soon," said Pidgeon, thinking of Margaret's long legs. "I hope."

Pidgeon was watching the nine o'clock news and wondering what the country was coming to. Strikes, inflation, work slowdowns, redundancies, a fire-bombing of two Jamaican shops in Newcastle, a cache of arms destined for some left-wing terrorist group found in a farmhouse near Slough, France beat Wales in rugby at Cardiff Arms Park. He was thinking that there were dark days ahead, plenty of them, when the doorbell rang. It was Margaret.

"Darling," she said, kissing him, "guess what?"

"What?"

"The King is a murderer." She laughed.

"How do you know?"

"I heard Noah on the telephone with Stanhope. Geoffrey, poor baby, was so upset he could hardly talk. He found the murder weapon. Missing the tip and everything."

"Christ," said Pidgeon.

"I've done my job," said Margaret.

"Yes?"

"Now you do yours." She smiled.

"I tried Sinclair again," said Smudge. "No luck. I think he's avoiding us." It was afterhours and the division room was emptying out. A knot of detectives stood by the door joking among themselves.

"I tried Sinclair again, too," said Pidgeon, leering. "And I think we've found our kukri."

"Get away," said Smudge. "I don't believe it."

"True. George VII, King of England, Scotland, Ireland, Wales, and a subscriber to *Country Life*, is our man. I'm telling you." Pidgeon looked delighted. Smudge did not.

"So now what? Swear out a warrant and stroll up to the palace?"

"Swear one out for Sinclair and Stanhope while you're at it. They're accomplices."

"Seriously, Tony. What do we do?" Smudge's voice reflected his anguish.

Pidgeon sighed. "I haven't got a clue."

"That's not unusual," said Harris, walking by.

That morning's *Times* was lying on the seat of the train that carried Huddleston home every evening. He had read the *Evening Standard* on the underground to Waterloo, so he didn't read *The Times* very closely. He glanced at Bernard Levin's column, but couldn't figure out what he was getting at. He turned to the section that listed the latest wills and bequests. He read that Dame Cynthia Platt of Rowley, Bucks, had left £126,640 to her heirs.

"Some people have all the luck," he said to himself.

He read the Court Circular with particular interest. His Majesty had met the Ambassador from Malawi in the morning and attended a luncheon for the Society of Illustrators in the afternoon. Captain Geoffrey Stanhope was also in attendance.

The King's brother, HRH Prince Victor Edward, the Duke of Moreland, had chaired the Royal Commission on Football Hooliganism.

Smudge looked away from the paper to the gray suburbs the train passed through. If they tried to question the King, what would happen? To Smudge the evidence "fit" well; but it was still circumstantial: he owned the murder weapon and he disappeared on the nights that it was used. *Could* you arrest the King? he asked himself. Smudge imagined you could. He'd be tried by the House of Lords, he supposed. If found guilty . . . he'd have to abdicate. What do you do with a murderous king? Send him to Wormwood Scrubs? Exile?

"God," said Smudge, in a whisper.

He turned back to the paper and studied the society page. There was a dinner that night for members of the Durbar Club at the private rooms of Blatchford's Hotel. Blatchford's, thought Smudge, very nice. Then a name caught his eye. *Sir Noah Sinclair, OM, will address the members.*

CHAPTER
ELEVEN

Blatchford's Hotel stands in Dover Street near Piccadilly, quiet, elegant, and a bit eccentric, like an elderly bachelor. It has catered to travelers of a certain class since the eighteenth century; it is world-famous, yet so unobtrusive as to be rarely noticed by pedestrians walking by.

Smudge was standing in front of the building when Pidgeon arrived.

"Any sign of him?"

"No," said Smudge.

"Been inside?"

"I took a stroll through the lobby. They looked at me as if I was not their usual type of clientele."

"Typical," said Pidgeon in disgust. He looked down the street. "Just what do we want out of Sinclair?"

"Some answers," said Smudge resolutely. "He was such a gent. I can't believe he'd treat us this way. I liked him. . . ."

"Do you honestly think he was ever on our side, Smudge? We were just an amusing afternoon to him."

"And you're just an amusing evening to his wife, right?"

It was about the most self-consciously nasty thing Smudge had ever said to him. Pidgeon colored. "That's different."

"Of course," said Smudge sarcastically.

Pidgeon looked up Dover Street and nudged Huddleston. "That's his car, isn't it?"

The gray Bentley came slowly down Dover Street and pulled gently up to the curb in front of the hotel, like a yacht. The doorman rushed out of the building, ignoring Huddleston and Pidgeon. In the car they could see Sinclair, a tiny reading lamp burning behind his shoulder, a book open on his lap. He looked up at the two policemen.

The doorman opened the door of the car.

"Good evening, Sir Noah. Good to have you with us once again."

"Thank you, Dalton," said Sir Noah, looking past the man to Smudge.

Glover opened the other door and unfolded Sir Noah's wheelchair, placing it on the pavement. As Huddleston and Pidgeon looked on, the chauffeur and the doorman reached into the car and took hold of Sinclair under the armpits. They lifted him awkwardly from the deep backseat and placed him in the wheelchair. Smudge could see Sinclair's legs, thin and atrophied, hanging like a child's limbs. Glover took his place behind the handles of the wheelchair and Dalton took charge of the small overnight bag.

"Good evening, Sir Noah," said Smudge, stepping up to him.

"Evening, Inspector." Glover stopped the chair.

"I wonder if you'd mind answering a few questions for us, sir?"

Sinclair sighed in exasperation. "I'm sorry, Inspector. I've given you all the help I can. You really must develop self-reliance, you know. You can't expect to be helped along every step of the way. You must excuse me."

Glover wheeled Sir Noah toward the door.

"Sir Noah . . ." Smudge began again.

But Sir Noah did not appear to have heard. He disappeared inside the hotel.

"Come on," said Pidgeon, making for the entrance.

"Why don't you leave the gentleman alone?" said Dalton, blocking the doorway.

"Why don't I punch your teeth in?" said Pidgeon hotly.

"Come on, Tony," said Smudge, pulling him away. "We'll get him later."

Pidgeon tore his arm free and took a few steps down the street.

"Come on," said Smudge, "I'll buy you a pint."

They found a pub on Sackville Street. Pidgeon didn't speak until he'd put away half his drink.

"What makes them better than us?" he asked quietly, but with a note of acid hate deep in his voice.

"Don't concern yourself, Tony. Finish your drink. We'll go back and get him later."

"He's got the accent and the money and the old school tie, and that makes him and his kind the lords of bloody creation."

"Things are a lot better now than they were," said Smudge.

Pidgeon turned on him angrily. "No, they're not any different. People think things are better now, more equal, fairer. But when it comes right down to it, if you're not one of them, you're nobody."

"Maybe," said Smudge, unwilling to provoke Pidgeon any further. They had another drink and stood at the bar in silence. After a while, Smudge finished up and said, "All right, let's have another go."

They reached Blatchford's and entered, Dalton hurrying from his glassed-in box to stop them. Smudge and Pidgeon showed their badges.

"Fetch Mr. Simms," said the aging desk clerk to Dalton, looking worried. "The night manager," he explained, his eyelids fluttering.

Mr. Simms came out of a side door, smoothing down his black waistcoat, walking through Blatchford's paneled lobby as if in a chapel. He was a portly man, with a smile born of years of diffidence frozen on his face.

"These gentlemen are from the police," said the desk clerk. "They would like to see Sir Noah."

"Thank you, Mr. Farmer. I'll handle this." Mr. Simms spoke just above a whisper. "Why don't you come into my office?" He smiled unctuously. "I'm sure we can sort this matter out...."

"We don't want to go into your office," said Pidgeon. "And if you try to prevent us from seeing Sir Noah, we shall have to run you down to West Central and charge you with obstruction."

"I see," said Mr. Simms. "Surely this matter can wait till morning. I'm sure Sir Noah would be glad to—"

"This matter can wait about another thirty seconds, Mr. Simms. And then I'll find Sir Noah and pull him out of his precious bloody Boy Scout meeting myself." Pidgeon was almost shouting.

Simms glanced around nervously. Dalton eyed the scene from his post.

"You must understand that the Durbar Club is a very formal organization. There are some extremely important people dining here this evening. I beg you not to create a scene...."

"I don't know," said Smudge. "I think we might have to call in some uniforms, Tony. Don't worry, Mr. Simms, we'll only bring half a dozen or so."

"Really, gentlemen!" said Simms.

"But you see," said Pidgeon slowly, "I'm not a gentleman, am I?"

Simms sighed. "Very well.... Dalton, show these gentlemen to the upstairs smoking room and I'll see if I can extract Sir Noah from the proceedings. I shall also need your full names and ranks. I'm sure the management will want to lodge a complaint with your superiors."

"Just go do some fast extracting," said Pidgeon, dismissing Simms.

They sat in the smoking room rather longer than they expected to. They had the room to themselves. Huddleston looked at the towering portraits of simpering eighteenth-century noblemen, and Pidgeon lit a cigarette.

126

"It's a smoking room, isn't it?" he said in reply to Huddleston's disapproving glance.

From down the hallway, they could hear the sounds of the dinner in progress: the clinking of cutlery, occasional bursts of laughter, a voice speaking above it, frequent shouts of "Hear! Hear!"

"What is the Durbar Club?" asked Pidgeon.

"An excuse for a beano, sounds like."

The door opened and Sinclair slowly wheeled himself in, a glowing cigar in his mouth. He was wearing white tie and tails; a few medals that looked like old coins were pinned on his breast, and a cross on a red ribbon dangled from his throat. He was smiling.

"You're making nuisances of yourselves," said Sinclair, as if speaking to children. Then he added, "Close the door, please, Huddleston."

Pidgeon stopped Smudge. "Close it yourself."

"Tony," said Smudge reproachfully. He disengaged himself and closed the door.

"Now, what is this all about?" Sinclair tapped his cigar in an ashtray.

"We might ask you the same question," said Smudge.

"Spare me your rather feeble sparring, Inspector."

"You've been withholding evidence," said Pidgeon.

"Have I? Who said so?" Sinclair's mouth twisted into a smile. His eyes twinkled.

"Never mind who."

"Is it true, Sir Noah, that you know who possesses a knife fitting the description of the murder weapon?" asked Smudge solemnly.

"No." He drew on his cigar.

"We know you do," said Pidgeon.

"How do you like my wife, Pidgeon? Pretty, isn't she?" He asked the question as if inviting him to admire a pedigreed hound or a thoroughbred.

"Very," said Pidgeon shortly.

"And you two get on well together?"

"Perfectly."

127

"But it never occurred to you that she might be leading you on with this ridiculous story?" He let loose a long, slow stream of blue smoke.

"It occurred to me." Pidgeon faced the older man tight-lipped and tense.

"And still you believe her?"

"Yes."

"Extraordinary." Sinclair leaned back in his chair. "Well, what Margaret has told you, between moans no doubt, is in fact true." He paused a second to let the words sink in.

"You admit it," said Smudge, aghast.

"Yes, I do. I don't like to lie to the police. No upstanding citizen does. But there again, no upstanding citizen would allow his loyalty to his sovereign to be questioned."

"Do you think the King. . . ?" asked Huddleston.

"Ah, Smudge," said Sinclair expansively, "that is not the question, is it?"

"What is?" asked Pidgeon coldly.

"The question is whether or not we should bother to find out if he is a rabid murderer of tarts."

"I can't believe this," said Pidgeon. "Just because he's the King doesn't mean he's above the law."

"Granted," said Sinclair, "the man is not exempt, but the office, the institution, is. Unfortunately, you can't take one away in a police van without removing the other."

"He should have thought of that before," said Pidgeon adamantly.

"Too late for that, I'm afraid," said Sinclair. "You should have realized that all this doesn't concern you." His voice had gone cold.

"For the first time, Sir Noah, you've hit the nail right on the head. The King doesn't concern me, and neither do you. I'm concerned with the murder of three tarts; and now that I have a fair idea who did it, I'm going to act," said Pidgeon slowly.

"Ah. A man of action! . . . It's not that simple." Sinclair felt for another cigar. "Has either of you a match?" he asked.

Pidgeon, in spite of himself, lit the cigar.

"I must ask you both to hear me out. This country, as I don't have to tell you, is in pretty poor shape. The men and women of this land have lost faith in everything, in their government, their industries, their great institutions. And why shouldn't they? They've been let down. Their government can't govern, their employers pay them enough to live about as well as the average Greek. . . . The only thing holding this leaky old vessel together is a rather handsome young man, with perhaps a somewhat bizarre but well-hidden flaw. His people love him. They have to; he's all they have left. Remove him and—well, I'm not sure what you have. Anarchy? Revolution? Who can say? Tell me, Smudge, you probably remember what it meant to be an Englishman once. Grand, wasn't it?" Sir Noah smiled broadly.

"Yes, sir," said Smudge dutifully.

"There was respect for us once, envy even. Now there is only bemused contempt and a certain admiration for our tailors. Do you want to contribute to that? Pidgeon, do you?" Sinclair seemed to rise a bit in his chair.

"I want to see justice done," Pidgeon answered stoutly. "Just for once, I want to see some bloke who's got a title pay for what he's done."

"Even if it's the grandest, most glorious title of all?"

"Especially that." Pidgeon stared down at the carpet.

"Where is the justice in depriving seventy million people of their self-respect? Hmm? Britain has never needed a king, a strong one, more than it does now."

"You make it sound as if he's bloody riding around on a white horse, urging us on. All he does is open sections of new motorways. My little sister could do that." A petulant tone had crept into his voice.

"But your little sister isn't exactly an inspiring figurehead." Sinclair was smiling again.

"Neither is the fairy queen who lives in the big house down the road," Pidgeon shot back.

"Tony . . ." cautioned Smudge.

"And after all, what are we saying he has done? Removed a

129

few undesirables. People we could do without."

"He chopped their guts out," said Pidgeon in disbelief. "He's a bloody animal."

"The modus operandi notwithstanding, I must ask you to drop this. It will lead to no good, for anyone."

"Not bloody likely," said Pidgeon.

"Smudge?" asked Sir Noah, raising his eyebrows.

"Well," he said, taking a deep breath, "I don't know."

"Perhaps this will convince you," said Sir Noah icily. "You retire in a few months, correct? I would hate to see you forced to retire early. Even with only six months to go, you'd find your pension cut by 40 percent. It would be a shortfall that you'd have to make up by continuing to work. Be hard finding a job at your age, wouldn't it, Smudge? It would be rather a shame, wouldn't it, to throw it all away?"

Smudge looked down at the floor as if he were going to cry.

"But," Sir Noah added brightly, "on the other hand, I'm sure rather a nice little bonus could be worked out if you were to see things our way. . . ."

"You bastard," said Pidgeon.

"As for you," said Sinclair, "you've got your whole career ahead of you. There's no telling how far you could go up—or down. I don't think I have to tell you how many friends I have. . . ."

"I won't do it."

"Well, whatever you do," said Sinclair, "you have to do it united. Because, Pidgeon, no one is going to believe your story without corroboration. I shan't help, of course. Neither shall Stanhope. Don't think Margaret will, Pidgeon. She needs you only for a service that she can find elsewhere. That leaves Smudge, here. I don't think you'll find a taker in him."

"I can't risk my pension, Tony."

"You can't risk your pension? Your bloody pension? What happened to 'I want to go out on top'?"

"I can't," said Smudge in agony. "I've got the wife to think of."

"I'll get you both *and* the bloody King," said Pidgeon quietly. He got up, and with a hate-filled glance at Huddleston stalked from the room.

Sir Noah and Huddleston sat in silence. Smudge stared at the floor, shoulders hunched. Sinclair smoked comfortably.

"Don't feel bad, Inspector. It's a very brave thing you're doing."

"Yes, sir. I suppose so." Huddleston rose. "I'd best be running along now, Sir Noah."

"Wait a minute, old boy," said Noah, grasping Huddleston lightly by the arm. "It's up to you now, Smudge. The nation doesn't know—it will never know—but you've got to hold this thing together. We've got a job to do, you and I. You keep Pidgeon from breaking ranks. I'll attend to the King." He smiled warmly. "You see, we can't afford a scandal."

"Yes, sir," said Smudge. "I understand that."

"Good. Very good." He paused a moment. "Now, you'll be sure to keep Pidgeon away from the palace. He can't go nosing around. . . ."

"I understand," said Smudge, glumly but dutifully.

"Excellent." Sinclair nodded. "I wonder, would you mind giving me a push down the corridor? Thanks so much."

Huddleston wheeled Sir Noah to a set of double doors at the end of the hallway. The sounds from within suggested that the party had grown more boisterous.

"Inspector," said Sinclair, tapping Huddleston on the hand, "on behalf of the country, I'd like to thank you."

"Just doing my duty, sir," said Smudge.

"You'll let me know if young Pidgeon gets a bit hard to handle. We'll see if we can't cool him down a bit."

"Yes, sir, of course, sir," said Smudge.

"Do me a favor—open the door. That's a good chap. I wish I could invite you in, but it's members only and you're not really dressed."

"I understand, sir. I'll miss my train if I don't hurry."

"Here, take a taxi." Sinclair felt for his notecase. "I insist, it's on me."

"That's not necessary, sir."

"Really, old fellow, I insist."

Sinclair thrust the note into Smudge's hand. "Capital. Now if you could just give me a shove. . . . Excellent."

"Noah!" said a voice in the room. "Where the devil have you been?"

"Eddie," said Sinclair, "I believe you're drunk."

"Damn drunk!" said Eddie.

The door closed and Smudge stood a moment and then made his way out of the hotel, giving the five pounds to Dalton. "For your trouble," he said.

Smudge walked down Dover Street to Piccadilly, past the Ritz to the Green Park tube station. At the head of the stairs leading down to the platform, he found Pidgeon leaning against the wall. Pidgeon's blond hair blew lightly in the perpetual breeze that sweeps London tube stations.

"Knew you'd come in here," said Pidgeon.

"Fancy a walk?" Smudge looked apprehensive.

Pidgeon looked at him with such hatred that he half expected him to assault him. "Not with you, mate."

"Come on," said Smudge, coaxing gently. "You'll feel better. You waited for me, didn't you?"

"Yeah, I waited. I just wanted to tell you that you're finished. You've had it. I'm going to put you away. No bloody pension . . . God, you make me sick." His voice echoed through the vast hallway.

"Tony, we'll talk about it on the street."

Reluctantly, Pidgeon allowed himself to be led off.

On the street, they walked toward Piccadilly Circus. Pidgeon seethed.

"You couldn't do enough to please him," he said suddenly, stopping to face Huddleston. "Your bloody lord and master. He wiped his boots on you and you just took it. Anything he wanted he could have. You just rolled over. . . ."

Huddleston's mustache seemed to droop, his shoulders sagged. They crossed Berkeley Street and Pidgeon continued his tirade.

"You put up with this shit your whole life. We all have. Anyone who doesn't have the right school behind them or the properly ancient money. And old Smudgie, good old Smudgie, Smudge 'I'll Do My Duty' Huddleston, just accepts his slap in the chops. Thank you, sir. Kick me in the arse, sir. Makes me sick, the whole bloody thing." Pidgeon kicked the curbstone. "What would good old upstanding Smudge Huddleston do if he found out that Jack wasn't the King of England but some poor bloody gas-fitter who lives in a semidetached house in Bermondsey? I'll tell you. Good old Smudgie would be round there quick as a flash with a warrant and a dozen uniforms and chuck the poor bastard in the Scrubs for the rest of his life. 'And, after all, what has he done?' " Pidgeon attempted an imperfect imitation of Sinclair. " 'Removed a few undesirables,' that's all. Christ . . ."

"Finished?" Smudge went through his pockets looking for his pipe. The wind blew out three matches before he got it lit.

Pidgeon shrugged his shoulders. They turned down St. James's Street.

"Because if you're finished, I'd like to say something."

Pidgeon shrugged his shoulders again. "Going to tell me about my duty?" he asked sarcastically.

"Yes," said Smudge, "I am. You've got this reputation around the office as being one of the tough new breed of copper. But I must say, Tony, you're not very bright. I mean, there you have Sir Noah Sinclair, our adversary—"

"My adversary. Your bloody master."

"And you tell him exactly what we're going to do. Oh, big man. Pound your chest. 'I'll get you, just you see!' Bloody stupid."

"You rolled over and died in there, Smudge. You couldn't grovel enough," Pidgeon spat back.

"No," said Smudge patiently. "That's what you think. That's what *he* thinks. But that was just a bit of playacting."

"Right," said Pidgeon.

"It was," Huddleston insisted. "He thinks I'm playing his game now. Doing what I'm told, like a good lad. He thinks I'm on his side."

"And you're not?"

"No."

"And what about your precious pension? Don't want the wife and kid to go hungry."

"I'm not worried. The only thing that worries me is that I've got such a bloody stupid partner," he said with a smile.

"Smudge, shut up."

"All my life," Smudge persisted, "I've been Smudgie, good old Smudgie. 'Don't worry, Smudge won't rock the boat.' 'He's a team player, is Smudge.' 'Smudge Huddleston, you can depend on him to keep his mouth shut.'" They passed St. James's Palace and the lone guardsman on duty, staring out from under his bearskin, followed them with his eyes.

"No more," said Smudge. "They've fed me their nonsense enough."

"Smudge . . ."

They turned into The Mall, heading west.

"We'll get him, Tony. We'll get them all."

"You're not having me on now, are you?"

"No, Tony. Starting now, the Metropolitan Police, the CID, Sir Noah Sinclair, and the bloody King himself will find themselves reaping the whirlwind in the form of Samuel Huddleston."

Pidgeon grinned. "You've gone round the bend, you have."

"No, I've just got a sense of purpose."

"Sense of purpose?"

"To catch Jack. Be he great or lowly."

They stood and stared at the floodlit bulk of Buckingham Palace.

"Not going to be easy," said Pidgeon.

"They have reckoned without the two finest lower-middle-class brains in London," said Smudge.

Pidgeon smiled. "And a copper out for revenge for a change."

Huddleston did not seem to have heard. He looked up at the palace, smiled, and said, "By the way, Tony, I have a plan."

CHAPTER
TWELVE

Hartley pounced on Pidgeon and Huddleston the moment they walked through the door of the office the next morning.

"You two, in here!" he shouted, his face dark as thunder.

"Let me just get a cuppa, Alf," said Pidgeon.

"Now!" Hartley demanded.

Pidgeon shot a glance at Smudge. "I think we've done something wrong," he whispered.

"Sit down," ordered Hartley. "And close the door."

A few men in the squad room saw the door to Hartley's office close and winked at one another. A closed door meant trouble.

"Okay," said Hartley. "What have you two got to say for yourselves?"

" 'Bout what?"

"Don't play the innocent with me, Tony. What were you two bastards doing at Blatchford's Hotel last night?"

"Making inquiries," said Smudge lamely.

"Who do you think you're talking to?" asked Hartley in disgust.

"Alf, what is going on?" asked Pidgeon.

"I'll tell you what is not going on," said Hartley. "I had a very pleasant little chat this morning with the Permanent Under Secretary of the Home Office."

"So?" said Pidgeon.

"So? So?" Hartley repeated irritably. "In case you have a false impression of my exalted position, Tony, I think you should know that the highest-ranking civil servant in the Home Office does not make a habit of ringing up a bleeding superintendent of police. Do you think he rang up just to see if I was getting on all right? Not likely. He phoned with a complaint against you and Smudgie. Some bloke I've never heard of, Sir Noah Sinclair, says that you've been bothering him."

"We weren't bothering him, Alf," said Pidgeon. "He had some information on this case, that's all."

"The permanent under secretary says differently."

"Does he?" said Pidgeon. "Well, let me tell you a thing or two, Alf. Me and Smudgie have turned up stuff on this case that you won't believe. . . ."

"Tony—" cautioned Smudge.

"What have you found?" demanded Hartley. "It seems to me that you've been sitting around doing sweet bugger-all on these killings and now you tell me that you're making police history."

Pidgeon took a deep breath, and was about to let the whole story go: Sinclair, the murder weapon, the King.

"Alf," said Huddleston quietly, "it's nothing. Tony was just shooting his mouth off."

Pidgeon, furious, looked at Huddleston.

"I don't believe you," said Hartley icily. "If you have information, I want to hear it."

"It's nothing," repeated Huddleston.

"Like hell," said Hartley.

The three men sat in silence for a moment.

"Okay," said Hartley finally. "If that's the way you want to play this game. You are both off the case—"

Pidgeon leaped to his feet. "What?"

"—and suspended. For two weeks. I'll give you that time to think this over. And if by then you haven't decided to tell me what the hell is going on, I'm starting proceedings against you both. Got it?"

"Alf," said Huddleston quietly, "I've never been suspended, not in over thirty years...."

"Sorry, Smudge," said Hartley coldly. "Tell me what you know or get out."

Slowly Huddleston got to his feet. "Okay, Alf, if that's the way you want it."

"I'm not the one making trouble for myself here, Smudge. I never would have thought in all my born days that you would withhold evidence from your bloody superior officer. I don't know what's come over you." Hartley sounded like a disappointed mother.

"See you in two weeks, Alf," was all Huddleston would say.

Huddleston changed a great deal in the next few days, so much so, in fact, that Irene worried about him constantly. Smudge went from being the solid, calm paterfamilias whom Irene had known for years to an edgy, withdrawn man, likely to jump at the sound of the telephone or a knock at the door. Furthermore, he had never slept past eight o'clock in his life no matter how late he had retired; now, after coming in at five in the morning, he often stayed in bed well past noon, lazing, reading the papers, and smoking his pipe. At six o'clock in the evening he went out. He did not say where he was going.

In the vaguest possible terms he told Irene about his suspension and would give no details; "a disagreement in the department" was all he would say.

But most surprising of all was Smudge's treatment of his son, Rodney. The boy was delighted when he heard of his father's trouble at work. One afternoon he casually made a remark about Huddleston's inability to hold down a job. Smudge listened for a moment, slowly took his pipe from his mouth, tapped it on an ashtray, and ordered his son out of the house.

"What?" asked Rodney in disbelief.

Smudge did not shout, but he was firm. "Come back when you learn some respect," he said.

137

The two faced each other for a second or two, while Irene looked on nervously. Instead of erupting into the howling she expected, Rodney colored to the tips of his ears and then stalked from the house. Smudge went back to his reading.

Huddleston went to Pidgeon's flat every night. The two men would have a bite to eat (Smudge was unresponsive to Pidgeon's more elaborate attempts at haute cuisine) and wait, sometimes dozing, sometimes watching television, until midnight. Then they would rise, conceal two walkie-talkies in their overcoats, and walk through the damp, empty streets to Buckingham Palace to begin their vigil.

There were three exits from the palace grounds: the main gate, the Royal Mews, and a curious little gate set in the wall at the far end of the park. The back door, they called it.

They ruled out the main gate, which was lit and guarded. They decided to concentrate on the Mews entrance in Buckingham Palace Road, although it was fairly well guarded, and the back door.

"What if there's a secret passage out of the palace?" Smudge asked suddenly one evening.

"Then we'll be standing out here for the rest of our lives."

Night after night they stood at their posts, Smudge at the Mews, Pidgeon at the back door, until 4:00 a.m., keeping in occasional radio contact. At four, they would stop in an all-night café near Victoria Station to have a cup of tea and talk over the case: when he came out, which way would he go? There were never any solid answers, just opinions, and as fatigue closed in on them they would fall silent, finish their tea, and head home. Smudge was spending a fortune on taxis.

Pidgeon stood in the lee of Wellington Arch, looking at the ponderous war memorials that littered the little green spot in the middle of the traffic circle. One night Smudge had pointed out to him the Royal Artillery Memorial, the RA having been Smudge's regiment during the war. He told Pidgeon that the white marble fieldpiece surmounting the monument was an-

138

gled so that if it fired a shell with enough power it would land in France.

"Good place for it," Pidgeon had said.

He looked around him continually, glancing occasionally at the back door. It was amazing the things you could see and hear at night: a couple strolling by on Hyde Park Corner having a row; two young bloods tearing down Park Lane in Jags, racing each other. Pidgeon watched their taillights disappear into Grosvenor Crescent and wondered if they would be caught by the E cars in Belgrave Square. He had just decided to switch his radio over to the traffic frequency, to find out, when he noticed, with a jolt, that the back door had opened. A figure dressed in dark clothes stepped out and made quickly for Knightsbridge. Pidgeon glanced at his watch: two-thirty. He changed the radio back to Smudge's frequency.

"Hello, Smudge, over," he whispered.

"Smudge here, over."

"He's on his way through the back door, over."

A burst of static. "No!" said Smudge. Pidgeon could imagine Smudge almost swallowing his pipe.

"He's heading for Knightsbridge. So am I."

"Keep me informed," said Smudge. "I'll be right behind you."

Pidgeon fell in about two hundred yards behind the King, praying that he would keep to the main streets. If he turned into Belgravia, Pidgeon wouldn't have time to catch up with him before losing George in the maze of side streets.

George passed the Hyde Park Hotel and Harrods. He turned left.

"He's going down the Brompton Road," Pidgeon said into the radio.

"Don't lose him," returned Smudge.

George strolled leisurely past the black bulk of the Victoria and Albert Museum and stopped to glance into the window of a bookstore in Cromwell Place.

"Where the hell are you going?" Pidgeon whispered to himself.

"Where now?" asked Smudge.

"Old Brompton Road, turning left again."

"He's in the wrong neighborhood," said Smudge, "for his kind of sport."

"I know that," whispered Pidgeon. South Kensington was not a red-light district by anyone's standards.

George turned into Onslow Gardens, a street of identical white-fronted row houses and residential hotels. George stopped in front of one, dug a key out of his pocket, and entered. A few seconds later the curtains were drawn in the front room of the second floor. A light went on.

"He's gone to earth," said Pidgeon into the radio; "26 Onslow Gardens."

"I'm on my way."

Pidgeon walked twice around the square, nervously puffing on a cigarette. He heard voices and footsteps, caught the flash of a hand lantern, and groaned to himself. A bloody police foot patrol.

"Good evening, sir," said one of the coppers.

"Live around here, do you, sir?" asked the other.

"No," said Pidgeon, "I don't." He dug in his pocket for his police card and held it up. "Why don't you two hop it?"

They shone a torch on the card and stepped back.

"Sorry, sir, no one warned us that you were working the area."

"I hope you haven't buggered it up," Pidgeon said.

"Sorry, sir," they said again and walked away.

"How were we supposed to know?" Pidgeon heard one say to the other.

"Bloody CID," his partner said.

A few minutes later Smudge entered the square, breathless.

"You know which flat?" he asked.

"Second floor." Pidgeon pointed to the lit window. "Now what do we do?"

"Haven't the foggiest idea," said Smudge.

"I doubt if he's up there doing anyone," said Pidgeon, dropping his cigarette to the ground.

Huddleston stared at the window a moment. "I think we'd better find out."

Using a credit card, Pidgeon easily slipped the lock of the front door of the building. "People wonder why they get robbed," he said in disgust. "A cocker spaniel could break into this place."

Smudge didn't answer. He was shining his torch on the mailboxes set in the wall. "J. Pratt," Smudge whispered. "Come on." Slowly they climbed the wide stairs covered in threadbare carpeting.

A woman opened the door of the second-floor flat only as wide as the chain lock would allow.

"Miss Pratt, is it?" asked Huddleston, peering through the crack.

The half of the woman's face that Smudge could see looked terrified. "Yes," she whispered. She was a strikingly beautiful woman, with dark hair and grayish eyes. Pidgeon assumed she was Irish—a lot of London prostitutes were. That is, if she was a prostitute.

"I'm Inspector Huddleston," he said softly, holding up his card. "This is Detective Pidgeon. May we come in?"

She closed the door and they heard the chain slide off.

The three of them filled the tiny entrance hall. "We believe a gentleman entered this flat a moment ago. I wonder if we might have a word with him?" Huddleston spoke as if he didn't want to wake anyone.

She looked pale and scared, her features showing plainly her fear of betrayal, scandal, ruin.

Pidgeon watched her closely, half expecting her to dash for the door or to overcome her terror with anger and order them out.

But she just sighed. "In there . . ."

Sitting on a sofa in a modest living room was the man whose face was on all the coins and stamps, bank notes and souvenir banners in England, the man Pidgeon had followed down the Brompton Road not fifteen minutes earlier.

"Your Majesty," said Smudge, supposing that the best way to start. Do you bow? he wondered.

"Are you from the police?" asked George.

"Yes," said Huddleston.

"I see," said George calmly. "Why don't you sit down."

The two policemen perched uncomfortably on the edge of their chairs. Both felt that it would somehow be disrespectful to lounge in front of the King.

"I presume you gentlemen have followed me here for a reason?"

"Well, actually, yes, sir, we have." Suddenly confronted with the man himself, Huddleston's resolve vanished.

Smudge was embarrassed, sure that he would be unable to say what brought him there. It was preposterous to think that the King was mixed up in any of this.

Pidgeon had no such doubts. "Are you armed, sir?" He used the tone of voice that Smudge supposed he would employ when talking to a vicar or an old lady.

"Good Lord, no."

"Do the names Marjorie Stewart or Brenda Pomeroy mean anything to you? Perhaps you knew Miss Stewart as Françoise?"

George stared at him blankly. "No, I'm sorry, I don't know those names. Perhaps if you gave me an idea of what this is all about . . ."

Pidgeon persisted, politely but firmly. "Can you give us an idea of your movements on the evening of November 6? Or November 30? Or December 14?"

George VII reacted to their questions like any civvy who had never had dealings with the police.

"I can't really say where I was."

Pidgeon looked at the woman. He had seen her before but he couldn't place her. "Do you have any idea, miss?"

The woman lowered her eyes. "He was with me." She had an American accent.

"Please," said George, "you don't have to tell them anything."

"If you were with this lady, sir, it might be in your interest to let her speak." Huddleston sounded unexpectedly stern.

"I think you had better explain what this is all about." There was the slightest note of annoyance in George's voice.

142

"Yes," agreed Huddleston, "I think I had." He drew a deep breath. "On three occasions in the past few months, sir, London prostitutes have been brutally murdered . . ."

As the story unfolded, the faces of George and the woman registered alternately shock, surprise, and, finally, fear.

"You mean to say," said George in disbelief, "that someone has killed these wretched women with a weapon that you have traced to me. . . ."

"Well . . ." said Smudge. He was reluctant to point out that there was no reason to suspect anyone other than George.

Pidgeon had not spoken for a while. He had listened to Smudge's careful retelling of the evidence against George, the nights out, the murder weapon, Stanhope's panicked confession to Sinclair (although Smudge had carefully left out any names), and realized that it all fit. Fit very nicely. But nothing works out that easily, Pidgeon told himself.

"Inspector," said George evenly. "I did not kill anyone."

"No," said Pidgeon, "I don't think you did."

"Neither do I, sir," said Huddleston hurriedly. "But proving it—"

"Smudge, I think that His Majesty has been set up."

Everyone stared at Pidgeon.

"Someone wants us to think that we've caught our Jack. Someone has found out about your nights out, sir, and has used that information to coordinate the murders."

"I can't believe it," said George.

"Well, it's an awful coincidence," Pidgeon shot back, and then remembered whom he was speaking to.

"Yes," said George, "I suppose it is."

Within Pidgeon's mind it all clicked quite suddenly. "We've been bloody stupid," he burst out.

Huddleston wished Pidgeon would watch his language in the King's presence.

"We've been played with by someone we thought had different motives altogether."

"Sinclair?" said Huddleston and then wished he could call the name back.

"Noah Sinclair?" asked George.

143

"Do you know him, sir?"

"He was warden of my college at Oxford. And he's the Regius Professor—he's appointed by the Crown. I don't see how he ties in."

"We heard about your ... activities and the knife from Sir Noah."

"But I told you," said the woman, "he was with me."

"Besides, who told Sinclair?" asked George heatedly.

Huddleston and Pidgeon exchanged glances. "You know a Captain Stanhope?" asked Smudge.

"Geoffrey would never—" George looked around the room quickly. "He's a very good friend of Sinclair's," he said quietly.

"Well," said Pidgeon, "as long as this lady says you were here ..."

"May I ask who you are, miss?" said Huddleston.

George interrupted. "No, you may not, Inspector. This lady ... this lady is married. I cannot allow her name to be dragged into this."

"She's your alibi, sir."

"If it comes to that, George, for God's sake ..." She sounded as if she were about to weep.

"This lady could be quite valuable to you, sir."

George shook his head. "I cannot allow it."

Huddleston didn't know what to say next.

"Inspector," said George, "you agree that I cannot have committed these murders."

"Yes, sir," said Smudge.

"And you?" George looked squarely at Pidgeon.

"It seems unlikely, sir."

"And you think that somehow Sir Noah Sinclair, or someone behind him, is trying to make me look like the culprit?"

"Yes, sir."

"That's how it looks from here, sir."

"And this lady cannot be dragged into it."

"That's what you say," said Huddleston slowly.

"Then we'll just have to try to nail Sinclair," said Pidgeon.

"Exactly," said George.

144

"Not a bad bloke, once you get to know him," said Pidgeon. They were walking through South Kensington toward Pidgeon's flat.

"A gentleman," said Smudge.

"Who do you think the woman is?"

"I know exactly who the woman is," said Smudge. He felt like a gambler with a handful of aces.

Pidgeon stopped. "Who?"

"I couldn't place her at first. Then, just as we were leaving, the penny dropped."

"For Christ's sake—"

"Her name is Jennifer Coughlin," said Smudge, pulling out his pipe. "She's the wife of the American ambassador."

Pidgeon's eyes grew wide. He whistled. "George is playing a very dangerous game."

"No wonder he hasn't married."

"Think what this would be worth to the papers . . ." Pidgeon laughed. "Just joking, Smudgie." They walked a block in silence.

The next morning Smudge was awakened by Irene. Through sleep-clouded eyes he stared up at his wife and realized that she looked as if she had seen a ghost.

"What is it, love?"

Irene said nothing. She handed him the morning paper. The heavy black type of the headlines shocked him fully awake: JACK STRIKES AGAIN!

He snatched the paper from his wife's hands, and read that the eviscerated body of Gloria O'Connor, a prostitute, had been discovered in a room in Romilly Street, Soho. The body had been found at half past four that morning. The account went on to mention that Detectives Huddleston and Pidgeon had been released from duty on the case and the investigation was now being conducted by Superintendent Alfred Hartley.

Smudge put aside the paper and lay back on his pillow. The King now had three witnesses to his alibi: Mrs. Coughlin and two members of the police force. Smudge smiled to himself. Sinclair had overplayed his hand.

"It was the same knife," said Pidgeon. The two men had met in a coffee bar in the Kings Road. Huddleston realized he was the oldest man in the tearoom.

"Right," said Smudge. "They're pushing us. One last murder to make us act."

"Why go through the charade at Blatchford's?"

"Reverse psychology. They wanted us to agonize over blowing the King's story, but they couldn't look too anxious about it." Smudge blew across his cup of tea to cool it.

"Why do you get rid of a king?" asked Pidgeon.

"To make someone else king," said Smudge.

"You've been giving this a lot of thought," said Pidgeon admiringly.

"Well, think it through," said Huddleston. "Sinclair and Stanhope have got plenty of money—Sinclair has, at least—so we can rule out simple blackmail. That leaves what? Power, I say. . . ." Smudge sipped his coffee.

"Power?" said Pidgeon. "The King hasn't got much direct power."

"Not on the face of it. . . . What was it that bloke said?—'The value of the Crown lies not in the power it wields, but in the power it denies to those who would abuse it.' In other words, remove the King and all hell breaks loose."

There was a long pause before Pidgeon asked the next question.

"How about Margaret? Where does she fit in?"

Huddleston laughed, and clapped Pidgeon on the shoulder. "Sorry, old chum, but I have a feeling she was a plant. She was a neat little bridge to the trail that led to the palace. You've been used, old son."

"Not for the first time," Pidgeon sighed ruefully.

146

CHAPTER
THIRTEEN

"This is a nine-millimeter, high-velocity, silencer model of the M-61 Skorpion machine pistol," said Jones, as if he were trying to sell one to Leary. "It can deliver one hundred and fifty rounds a minute in almost total silence. Here, hold it."

He passed the gun to Leary, who caressed it lovingly. It was no longer than his forearm and it nestled against his chest comfortably.

"I'll take you out for practice later," said Jones, "but remember, the actual shooting is the least important thing you'll have to do. Getting in position is the hardest part and that is what this training has been all about."

"We're getting close," said Flynn, smiling. "How do you feel?"

"On top of the world," Leary answered, cradling the gun.

"Good fellow," said Flynn. "Now pay attention."

Jones unfurled a floor plan on the table. "This is a plan of the cellars of the Dorchester. You know where it is, don't you?"

"No," said Leary.

"It's a hotel in London. That is where the job is going to take place."

"Won't there be a lot of people around?" asked Leary.

"Not a soul. Now listen. You will enter the hotel at approximately half past six in the morning, through the tradesmen's entrance on Deanery Street. Either Flynn or I will drop you off. You'll be carrying a tray of rolls for the kitchen. Don't worry about being seen—between six and nine it's like a bloody invasion down there. Hundreds of deliveries . . ."

"Right," said Leary.

"Walk past the storage rooms here." He pointed on the map. "Then to the pastry kitchen here—but don't go in, keep on going. Past the employees' canteen to these stairs leading to the subbasement. At the bottom of the stairs are four doors, numbered 1 through 4. Go into number 4. Got it, 4?"

"Four," said Leary. "But when does the shooting start?"

Harris met Huddleston and Pidgeon in a pub in Petty France. He came in obviously in a great hurry and looking concerned.

"Hullo, Lennie," said Pidgeon. "How's work?"

"What's this all about? I could get shopped for meeting you two in a pub during working hours."

"I wouldn't worry," said Huddleston.

"Don't give it a moment's thought," said Pidgeon reassuringly. "Listen, Lennie, we've got a little surprise for you. . . ."

"What?" asked Harris, his eyes narrowing.

"A promotion," said Pidgeon. "We just made you chief inspector."

"What are you going on about?"

"We can't give you too many details," said Smudge mysteriously, "but you have to do a little playacting for us."

"Namely," put in Pidgeon, "become Chief Inspector Harris."

"Impersonate a higher-up? Not bloody likely," said Harris, rising. "Bugger up my whole career, that would. . . ."

"You haven't got a career," said Pidgeon through clenched teeth.

"Tony," cautioned Smudge. "Sit down, Lennie. . . . Now,

148

look, we have to put a tap on someone's line—not in London, in Oxford—and you can bet that the local lads will check the authorization back through the Yard."

"You can't get a tap without a magistrate's permission," protested Harris.

"And we've got it. It's right there on Chief Inspector Harris's desk," said Pidgeon.

"I can't do it," said Harris firmly.

"Lennie, you've got to," Smudge pleaded, "or we'll never get back on the force."

"You'll be coming back just as I'm leaving."

"Look," burst out Pidgeon, "we wouldn't ask you to do this if it wasn't bloody important, would we?"

"No," agreed Harris, "but—"

"And you know what we've been working on. You know that this might help us catch the loony that's carving up these birds."

"Yes," said Harris, "but Alf—"

"Bugger Alf," said Pidgeon.

"Lennie," said Smudge quietly, "you're our only hope. . . ."

"We'll take full responsibility," said Pidgeon.

"Bloody marvelous." Harris looked as if he might be in pain. "Okay, lads, you've got yourself a chief inspector."

"Super," said Pidgeon.

"How about buying me a drink?"

"What?" asked Smudge. "On duty?"

The telephone in Pidgeon's flat rang and Smudge picked it up; he knew exactly who it would be.

"Okay, Smudgie," said Harris, "the Oxfordshire constabulary have agreed to put the tap on your bloke's line. Tony says it'll be in place this afternoon. Anytime after two o'clock."

At two-twelve that afternoon Sinclair took Huddleston's call.

"How is our man in the front line?" asked Sinclair.

"Not too good, Sir Noah. It's Pidgeon. The last murder really ly set him off. I don't think I can hold him."

"Inspector," said Sinclair gravely, "I've explained all this to you. You simply have to hold him. For the good of the country."

"I know that, sir," Huddleston protested, "but—"

"What does he plan to do?" Sinclair interrupted irritably.

"Go to the press, sir."

"Can you give me any idea of when?"

"I don't know exactly, sir. Tomorrow, perhaps. Maybe the day after."

"He'll be in serious trouble if it's tomorrow." Sinclair chuckled. "That's the day of the Royal Christmas reception."

"I don't know anything about that, sir."

"No," said Sinclair, "you wouldn't."

A half mile away from Sinclair's study, Pidgeon and a technician, in a Post Office telecom van, heard the conversation end.

"Line dead," said the technician. And then, a few seconds later, "Line alive."

The clicking of the telephone dial crackled through Pidgeon's headset.

"London number," said his companion knowledgeably. Into the headset microphone angled in front of his mouth, he said, "Trace, please. London."

They could both hear the sounds of a phone ringing, very far off, it seemed.

"Beaumont House," said a properly servile voice.

"Sinclair here."

"One moment please, Sir Noah."

A few seconds later the phone was picked up again. "Noah, why haven't you phoned?" The voice was most agitated.

"What am I doing now, Eddie?"

"Never mind," said Eddie, annoyed.

"The show is on for tomorrow."

"Christ! We'll all be at the palace."

"Don't worry, Eddie."

"Nothing will go wrong?" Fear replaced anger.

"I've never failed you, have I, Eddie?"

150

"Don't start now," said Eddie glumly.

"I'll be in touch."

Pidgeon lit a cigarette.

"What's this all about?" asked the technician, pushing the mike away from his mouth for a second.

"Jewel thieves," said Pidgeon.

The man looked impressed. "They planning a big job?"

"The Crown Jewels," said Pidgeon, without cracking a smile. "But don't you breathe a word. If this gets out, we'll know who told them."

"Honest, never, I wouldn't," said the man earnestly. The man held his earphone and wrote on a pad in front of him. "Thank you, London." He passed it to Pidgeon. "Here's your first number."

"Thanks." He glanced at it.

"Line alive," the man said.

The clicking began. "London again."

"Astley," said a voice.

Astley? thought Pidgeon.

"Randolph? Noah here. Everything's set for tomorrow."

"How clever you are," said Astley.

"Line dead," said the technician. "London?" he said into the microphone. "Here's your second number."

"Thanks," said Pidgeon.

"Line alive," said the technician. "Not London this time."

"Where?" asked Pidgeon.

"Don't know yet. . . . London, can you take this line on trace? Righty-oh. . . . Going through the Aberdeen exchange." And then, in case Pidgeon confused it with another Aberdeen, "In Scotland."

"I've heard of it," said Pidgeon.

"London?" asked the technician. "What's going on?" He nodded. "He's gone on radio patch," he said to Pidgeon.

"Hullo?" said a voice.

"Sinclair here."

"Yes, sir."

"I think it's time to get your man in position. Is he ready?"

Pidgeon noted a touch of pride in the voice. "Oh, yes, sir,

he's ready. I had my doubts at first, but he's taken to the work very well. He handles a weapon like he's been doing it all his life."

"And he doesn't suspect who you actually are?"

"He thinks he's striking a blow for a free Ireland, bless 'im. He hasn't a clue who the Coughlins are, though."

Pidgeon stiffened. The Coughlins were targets. Of course, he told himself; remove Jenny, and George was without an alibi. Or so Sinclair thought.

"You'd better come down to London immediately."

"We're on our way, sir."

"Excellent. You've all done excellent work. The show is on for tomorrow. You must have your man in place by noon."

"He'll be there with time to spare."

"Excellent," said Sinclair.

"Line dead," said the technician. And the line stayed dead for an hour until Sinclair's cook called the local butcher to order a Christmas turkey.

Two Scottish police Land-Rovers moved bumpily over the track that led out to the farmhouse buried deep in the Grampians near the village of Fechan. It was dark and the vans traveled without lights, hoping to catch anyone lurking at the house unawares. There was a certain amount of grumbling in the party.

"Scotland Yard whistles so we have to jump," said Inspector Ackroyd, in the lead van. It had taken them several long, cold hours to find the place. "Chief Inspector bloody Harris," he muttered.

The cottage was a damp-looking dark spot in the gloom. "There it is," said Ackroyd. He unclipped his radio from the dashboard. "Hector," he told the driver in the rear car, "take your lads round the back. We're going in the front door. And let's keep quiet."

The Land-Rovers stopped, and the men scattered into the night. Ackroyd and a uniformed officer walked to the front door. He knocked forcefully. There was no answer. The officer peeked in the window.

"Can't see a damn thing."

Ackroyd softly turned the door handle. The door opened slightly. Gingerly he nudged it farther.

"Police," he called into the gloom. There was silence within.

"There's nobody here," he said. "Give me the torch."

He switched on the torch and shone it around the empty living room. A folding table stood in front of the window and a camp chair was set up in front of the fireplace.

"Bring them in, Sergeant," said Ackroyd, with an air of resignation.

The sergeant blew an ear-piercing blast on his whistle.

Ackroyd winced. "I had hoped you might use the radio."

"It's all right, lads, there's no one here," shouted Ackroyd. "Give the place a thorough going-over and let's get home." He lowered himself into the camp chair as his men scurried through the four tiny rooms.

"Take a look around outside, too," said Ackroyd to no one in particular. "Of course," he added conversationally, "I don't really know what we're looking for. Or who."

"Clean as a whistle," said Gough.

"Nothing," said Mackay.

"Did you check there?" said Ackroyd, swiveling his torch toward the grate.

An officer dropped to his knees and rummaged through the cold ashes in the fireplace. "There's nothing here, Inspector," he said, looking in dismay at his soot-covered hands.

"I expected you to say that," said Ackroyd. "I think."

Harris listened to Ackroyd's sad tale over the phone, clucking every so often in sympathy at the Scottish officer's having come up empty-handed. "Happens to us all, Inspector. Pay it no mind. . . ."

Ackroyd kept talking.

"Thanks, Inspector," he said, smiling now into the phone. "I owe you one, thanks. . . ." He hung up, sighed, and immediately dialed Pidgeon's number.

"Not a damn thing up there. Clean as a whistle . . ." said Pidgeon.

"They're very professional, Sinclair's lads," said Smudge.

"I'm glad you admire our noble foe," said Pidgeon sarcastically. "In the meantime, Sinclair's lads are on their way to London, disguised as bloodthirsty IRA gunmen, looking to kill the American ambassador's wife—who is, coincidentally, the alibi for the King of England."

"They've got guts," said Smudge. "I'll grant them that. . . . This Irish business is pretty farfetched, isn't it? They'd have to be going after him, not her. He's the one who's made enemies in the North—least that's what the papers say."

"So maybe that's it."

"What do you mean?"

Pidgeon sat back in his chair. "Sinclair is only interested in getting rid of Jennifer. But to throw everyone off, he'll probably kill the ambassador as well, and make it look as if he were the target. She just gets caught in the cross fire. Perfect setup, really."

"It's clever. . . ." said Smudge. He got up and wandered into the kitchen to make some tea. He had begun to treat Pidgeon's flat as though he lived there. "You heard Sinclair say they had to make their move by noon tomorrow," Smudge called out as he filled the kettle.

"Surely the Coughlins will be going to that party whatnot at the palace," Pidgeon shouted back.

"Probably. We could check that." Smudge returned from the kitchen.

"So, if they are sending someone down to do them in . . ."

"Look," said Huddleston, straightening up, "they can't get them at the hotel. You've got the American security lads upstairs, the DPG downstairs. And they would be bloody stupid if they tried anything on the route to the palace."

"You don't suppose they have anyone inside the palace, do you?" said Pidgeon.

"Seems unlikely." Huddleston shrugged. "I mean, if they could get someone in, they could never get him out."

Pidgeon swept his hair back off his forehead, an impatient gesture. "So where, then?"

"You realize, of course," said Huddleston slowly, "that we have information regarding the possible assassination of two very important people and we haven't notified anyone about it. You do realize that, don't you, Tony?"

Pidgeon stared at Huddleston blankly.

"You haven't heard a word I've said, have you?" asked Huddleston petulantly.

"The lift," said Pidgeon suddenly. "They'll hit them in the lift." He jumped to his feet.

Huddleston spent a fitful night, deathly worried. Irene read the stress on her husband's face, and although she disapproved of the strain he was putting on himself, she said nothing, not even when he slipped out of bed in the depths of the night to make himself some cocoa. She awoke when the alarm clock rang a few hours later; he was gone.

"Not fair on him," she said aloud. "At his age . . ."

Smudge almost seized Pidgeon by the lapels when he arrived at the flat that morning. "We have got to tell the DPG," Smudge insisted.

"No, we don't," said Pidgeon blandly. "I've got it all worked out. . . ."

"What are we going to do?" Smudge's face was pasty white from lack of sleep.

The downstairs doorbell rang. Smudge jumped. Pidgeon spoke into the intercom.

"Postman," said the voice on the street. "Registered letter. You have to sign."

"Shan't be a minute, Smudge," said Pidgeon. He was back moments later, staring at his letter.

155

"Take a look at this."

"Never mind that," said Smudge feverishly, "what's the plan?"

"What plan?"

"About the Coughlins. You said you had it all worked out."

"Calm down, Smudgie." Pidgeon grinned. "First we have a cup of tea. . . ."

"Tony," groaned Smudge.

"Then we fit ourselves out with some ordnance."

"Guns?" said Smudge. "I don't have a gun."

"I have."

Smudge looked deeply worried. "We don't need guns, Tony."

"We've got to protect Mrs. Coughlin. And Mr. Coughlin, too, for that matter . . ."

"The DPG," protested Smudge.

"Bugger the DPG." He flipped the letter at Smudge. "Take a look at this."

It was an invitation to the Royal Christmas reception. And a note: "As all the principal players in this little drama will be under one roof today, I think you should be there." It was signed simply "George."

"Oh, Lor'," said Huddleston.

CHAPTER
FOURTEEN

A baker's van with Jones at the wheel pulled up in front of the service entrance of the Dorchester on Deanery Street. Leary, dressed in white overalls, stepped out of the double doors of the back. He shouldered a tray of rolls and walked into the hotel whistling.

"Marvelous," said Jones as he put the van in gear and drove away.

The labyrinthine corridors of the basement were crowded with members of the early shift coming on duty and the late shift finishing up. A couple of room-service waiters joked in the passageway, waiting for the seven-o'clock morning rush to get under way. No one paid any attention to Leary, despite his rather peculiar way of walking. The silencer of the machine gun was taped to the side of his chest and the gun itself ran down his thigh.

He followed his instructions to the letter. In the basement, he found the door leading to the base of the number 4 shaft. "That Jones is a clever bloke," Leary said to himself.

He swung the door open and slipped inside. The tiny room was greasy and dark. Directly above him, three or four floors, he reckoned, was the lift. Right in front of him was the anchor, a cable running from the base of the car to the floor of the building to hold the car steady.

He dumped the rolls on the floor, stripped off his overalls and shirt, and unstuck the pieces of the gun from his chest, wincing as the tape pulled at his chest hair. He dressed again quickly, slung the gun over his back, slipped on a pair of canvas gloves, and stared at the side of the wall. Metal rungs, just like the one in the cave, protruded from the shaft wall. He glanced at the watch Jones had given him: 7:40 a.m. He started to climb.

In his suite Coughlin was wrestling with his tie and worrying about making a mistake in front of the King.

"My love," said Jennifer, "you've done it before. This won't be nearly as hard as the coronation or presenting your credentials."

"Yes," said Coughlin, "but I'm always afraid I'll forget some little detail."

"You bow your head, call him 'Your Majesty' the first time, and 'sir' after that. You introduce me—"

"It's ridiculous. I've met him before. You've known him for years, since college."

"I know, I know, but it has to be done this way."

"You certainly know a lot about it."

"I've had a lot of time to practice."

He kissed her on the forehead. "I'm glad my daddy isn't alive to see a Coughlin getting friendly with a King of England."

"He'd be proud," said Jennifer.

"Like hell," said Coughlin. "Like hell."

Charlie Leary sat on the roof of the number 4 car eating a packet of ham sandwiches that Jones had prepared for him. It was eleven o'clock and he was a little bored and a little nervous, like an actor before his cue.

He meticulously picked a slice of cucumber from his sandwich and threw it against the back wall of the elevator shaft. It stuck there. He picked out another piece and threw it. It stuck. He took another bite, and as he chewed he noticed the pieces of cucumber starting, very slowly, to slide down the wall.

"Racing," he said, with his mouth full, and began rooting for the piece he had thrown first.

As the other lifts worked up and down in their shafts, he could hear people talking. The lift machinery stopped and started with a little screech, a noise that was getting on Leary's nerves. He watched the counterweight for the number 3 glide silently by.

He ran through his instructions again. At approximately twelve o'clock the ambassador, his wife, and a security agent would get into the lift. He was to let the car drop two floors and then stop it, using the key. He tapped his breast pocket.

"Key," he said.

Then he was to open the hinged housing holding the fan on the roof, leaving a large hole in the ceiling of the lift. Shoot the occupants. Climb down the rungs, call the number, find out where the money was. And then get on his Pan Am flight to New York that night.

The choice of destination had been Leary's. He reasoned that there would be plenty of work for a man with his skills in a city like New York.

In Leary's trouser pocket was another key. It opened a suitcase. The suitcase was in a left-luggage office in one of the London railway stations. The claim stub was taped under a telephone in a phone box somewhere in London. When he called to report that the job had been carried out, they'd tell him which phone box had the ticket in it. The suitcase had his money, a passport, an airline ticket, "and a few things you'll need in America," Jones had said.

Leary sighed and rested his head on his drawn-up knees. He was a bit disappointed in his target. He had been hoping for a member of the Royal Family at least.

———

The Sinclair Bentley was stuck in traffic on the North Circular Road, the main approach to London.

"Glover," said Sinclair, "we aren't going to be late, are we?"

"No, Sir Noah." Glover kept his eyes fixed on the rear end of the Austin Marina in front of him.

"Tell me something, Noah," said Margaret matter-of-factly. "Do you honestly expect this harebrained scheme to work?"

Sinclair smiled the bland Buddha smile that had infuriated students and prime ministers for decades. "Have you ever known me to fail at anything?"

She lit a cigarette and exhaled, the smoke flattening itself against the side window.

"And," continued Sinclair, "I wouldn't call it harebrained. Bizarre, perhaps. Extraordinary, maybe. Brilliant, actually."

"But it won't work," she insisted.

"Oh," he said bluntly, "it'll work. Right now, as we speak, Freddie is prepared to back us with the army and Wilfred is behind us with the navy. The RAF is a bit touchy. Quentin has always been a bit of a trouble spot—as far back as Eton."

"Freddie and Wilfred are asses."

"You're talking about the Chief of Staff and the First Sea Lord," said Sinclair, smiling. "What's your impression of the Air Marshal?"

"Quentin?" said Margaret. "He's an ass, too."

"But their hearts are in the right place," said Sinclair.

'Britain isn't a banana republic," said Margaret indignantly. "You can't just use the armed forces to take control."

"Brilliant, my dear," said Sinclair jovially. "Why do you think we've gone to such lengths to blacken our good King's name? People rally round a king, not around some cheap Labour politician from Scunthorpe. Let's face it, there's an almost feudal faith in the Crown. Destroy that and in the commodious British heart there will be a deep longing for a nice clean slate and a new crowned head. I think the whole thing is devilishly clever, actually."

Sinclair rapped on the glass. "Glover, would you get this damn thing moving?"

Glover's eyes narrowed under his visor. "Yes, Sir Noah."

"You're looking forward to this, aren't you?" Margaret stubbed out her cigarette.

"Yes, I am rather. It's a bloodless coup, designed by me—"

"Not quite bloodless. Was it three or four whores?"

"Four," said Sinclair. " 'Four and whore rhyme aright, so do three and me, I'll set the town alight.' "

"What the hell is that?"

"It's a bit of poetry," said Sinclair airily. "Jack the Ripper's only known foray into verse. Shall I go on?"

"No," said Margaret. "You know, you're not the man I married."

"Neither is Pidgeon," said Sinclair gleefully.

Donning his court uniform, Sir Randolph Astley looked at himself in the mirror and hoped that the coming events of the day wouldn't be too unpleasant. Noah had sworn that it was a foolproof plan.

He looked once again at the television page and noted with satisfaction that *Dallas* was a two-hour special that night.

At Beaumont House, HRH Victor Edward looked at his wife.

"You know, Bessie," he said, "I never really wanted to be King, but Noah says it's for the good of the country. And, damn it all, George is a good sort, but he's just not getting the job done."

"Yes, dear," said Bessie, who wanted to be Queen rather badly.

Deep within him, George could feel little but cold fury. He had acted rashly, he knew—by starting things up with Jennifer after so many years—he had risked everything. But to have his weakness exploited by the people around him, the very people he trusted and needed, was unforgivable. Thank God for those two policemen. They were his only hope now, the only people—apart from Jennifer, of course—that he could trust. It would all be over today, he told himself. And then there would be hell to pay.

Leary watched the seconds tick away. It was twelve o'clock: any minute now.

The number 3 lift swept by him on its way to the top floor. He listened intently for the sounds of the number 4 door opening. He tensed and opened the hatch an inch or so. A man in a dark suit had stepped into his lift.

Security. Leary checked him off in his head.

Another man entered. The ambassador.

And a woman. What a knockout, thought Leary. His key was in place.

"What time is it?" asked the ambassador.

"Just after twelve—one minute past, sir."

"Right on time," said Coughlin.

The door closed and the lift started moving. One floor, Leary counted.

The number 3 lift was just above them. Leary took a deep breath and reached to turn his key. As he did so, he glanced at the roof of the car which had drawn alongside in the next shaft. Two men with guns stood there. One held his gun confidently, the other less so, but both were pointing them at Leary.

"Hullo," said Pidgeon softly, winking.

CHAPTER
FIFTEEN

The two lifts rode side by side to the ground floor, Leary all the while unsure of exactly what to do. If he carried out the job, the two policemen would undoubtedly shoot him; if he shot the policemen, he knew that he would probably be killed by the security man in the lift. While pondering all this, the cars stopped at the lobby level and Leary felt his car wobble a bit as the Coughlins got out.

Without taking his eyes off Leary, Pidgeon called out, "Lennie?"

"Hullo?" Harris called from within the number 3 car.

"Get in the number 4 lift and take it up to eight."

Smudge pressed eight on the roof board of their car, and both rose again.

"Now," said Pidgeon to Leary, "you lay your gun down on the roof. Very good."

"Prisoner of war," said Leary in a whisper.

"What?" asked Pidgeon.

"Prisoner of war, copper," Leary said. "I'm a bloody prisoner of war."

"I'll give you prisoner of war, paddy. What's your name?"

Leary was silent, scared.

Pidgeon pumped his gun. He had gone red in the face from anger, and Smudge, who didn't like firearms, was genuinely afraid that Pidgeon was going to take a shot at the man.

"What's your bloody name, paddy?"

"Leary," said Leary.

"All right, Leary. How did you get here?"

"I'm not telling you a bloody thing. I'm a prisoner of war."

"Prisoner of war?" said Pidgeon. "What army?"

Leary pulled himself up straight. "The Irish Republican Army."

Huddleston and Pidgeon exchanged glances. It was the set-up they had expected—except that they didn't think that the killer would try to pitch it to them.

"What were your instructions?"

Leary sat on the roof, his arms folded, as if awaiting a long-overdue bus.

"Lennie?" called out Pidgeon.

"Hullo?"

"Take it up."

"Right."

"You've got one floor, Leary," said Pidgeon.

There were only nine floors in the building. Less than a foot above the ninth in the elevator shaft was a metal grate protecting the winch housing for the lift.

"You're going to make an awful mess, Leary."

Smudge saw what Pidgeon was going to do. "Tony, for God's sake!"

Leary looked up, suddenly aware that there wouldn't be enough room for him between the lift roof and the grate. He flipped open the fan housing and saw Harris and Harris's gun.

Leary's arched back touched the grating. He flattened himself on the roof.

"All right! All right! Jesus!"

"Hold it, Lennie," called Pidgeon. "Take it down."

Huddleston heaved a sigh of relief. "Tony, you crazy bastard."

164

Leary's chest was heaving as they hustled him off the elevator roof, through the car, and into a service station on the ninth floor.

Pidgeon pushed Leary up against the wall. "Talk."

"It was a fella named Flynn and one named Jones," he said breathlessly.

"Who?"

"They recruited me. Trained me . . ."

"And?"

"I was supposed to kill everyone in the lift."

"And?"

"Make a call. I've got the number here." His hands trembled as he pulled the piece of paper from his pocket.

Huddleston snatched it from his hand. "Lennie," he said, "get a location on this number."

"And?" Pidgeon demanded.

"I'd tell them that I did the job and they'd tell me where to pick up my money."

Pidgeon threw him toward the door. "You're going to make that call, Leary."

Harris, Huddleston, and Pidgeon watched as Leary dialed the number from the security room downstairs. The number rang once.

"Leary," he announced.

"Where the hell have you been?" Jones barked.

"Taking a walk, unwinding," Leary lied easily. He didn't owe them anything now. He had never liked that Jones character.

"How did it go?"

"Worked like a charm."

"How do you feel?" Leary thought he could detect a note of affection in Jones's voice.

"Top of the world," said Leary.

"Now listen carefully, 'cause I'm going to say this once. The ticket stub is in a box at the Savile Row end of Burlington Gardens. The suitcase is in Paddington Station. Got it?"

"Yes," said Leary.

"You've done a good job, Leary."

"Thanks," said Leary, and hung up.

"He did it," said Jones jubilantly. Flynn smiled. "I don't bloody believe it."

"Calls for a celebration," said Flynn.

"Damn right."

A car slid quietly into the street and stopped next to the two men. Jones looked at the four occupants and knew that, as he had feared all along, Leary hadn't done it. He started to run as the car doors opened.

"Don't do that," said one of the men, "or we'll have to do you for resisting arrest."

Jones and Flynn turned around and got into the car, quiet and ashen-faced.

"What's your name?"

"O'Brian," said Flynn.

"And you?"

"Montague," said Jones.

"Can you prove that? Got a license or something?"

Both men reached for their inside pockets. "Slowly," said one of the policemen. They produced army identification.

"Regimental Sergeant Major Harold Montague," the policeman read out. "And Color Sergeant James O'Brian."

"Come on," said the man driving.

"Don't believe it," said the man next to him.

"True," said their companion. "And they're both Royal Hussars."

"Shame and dishonor on the regiment," said the driver.

"Conduct unbecoming," said the man next to him.

"I've torn my trousers," said Smudge in alarm as the squad car carrying them to the palace turned on its sirens. "On the roof of the lift."

"You can hardly see it," said Pidgeon.

166

"I can't go to bleeding Buckingham Palace with a tear in my trousers!"

"Keep your coat on," said Pidgeon.

Harris, driving, killed the siren on The Mall. "We don't want to alarm anyone, do we? By the way, you must have noticed by now that I haven't asked a single question about what's going on."

"You're not getting any answers," said Pidgeon.

"I don't want answers," said Harris, "I just wondered if you had noticed."

They stopped at the gates of the palace and a policeman checked their invitations against identification. He gave them a funny look as they drove into the palace courtyard.

"He noticed my trousers," said Smudge.

"He's just wondering what a bunch of coppers are doing showing up at an affair at the palace."

"Actually," said Harris, "he probably did notice your trousers. I hear they're trained to spot things like that. . . ."

The first person Sir Noah Sinclair saw upon entering the state reception room at Buckingham Palace was Sir Randolph Astley.

Sir Randolph was at the far end of the lavish, gold-encrusted room, but he made for Sinclair immediately. It was not an easy progress. The room was crowded with people, some known to Astley, others completely unknown. There were dozens of citizens of former imperial colonies, some dressed as conservatively as City bankers, others wearing their native dress, swirling bright robes and feathers or voluminous saris.

From the ceilings hung huge chandeliers, brightly lit, for little light was cast through the tall windows from the gray winter day outside. The walls were lined with historical paintings so large it was hard to figure out exactly which glorious feat of British arms they depicted.

"Noah," said Astley, bending to shake Sinclair's hand, "how good of you to come."

"Wouldn't have missed it for the world, Randolph," said

Sinclair. And then quickly changed his mind. A few feet ahead of him in the crowd, standing with her husband, was Jennifer Coughlin.

"Damn," he said. He tapped Margaret's hand. "From here on, my dear, things could become rather unpleasant."

"Why?" asked Margaret. She was wondering if there was someplace she could smoke a cigarette.

"Because someone has blundered," said Sir Noah icily.

"How Tennysonian of you, darling."

At one o'clock the band segued from an Elgar romance into "God Save the King," and George entered the room, attended by Victor Edward and his wife, both looking rather nervous, and Stanhope. A few Yeomen of the Guard, Gentlemen at Arms, and Gentlemen Ushers unobtrusively divided the crowd into two blocks, one on either side of the room, and George began working his way down the middle. He was being introduced to his guests by the Lord Chamberlain.

"The Prime Minister of Mauritius, Your Majesty," the chamberlain whispered discreetly.

"Your Majesty," said the prime minister.

"Yours is a lovely country," said George, smiling. "How lucky you are to be able to live there."

"Indeed, sir," said the Prime Minister of Mauritius.

"The American ambassador, Your Majesty."

"Mr. Coughlin, how wonderful to see you again."

"Your Majesty," said Coughlin, bowing. "May I present my wife."

"Your Majesty," said Jennifer, curtseying.

George progressed down the line, greeting prime ministers, ambassadors, and other dignitaries. Some handled themselves quite well and others simply gibbered, their smiles frozen on their faces. George didn't think less of them if they didn't quite carry it off. He'd seen it so many times before.

"Sir Noah Sinclair," said the chamberlain.

"Sir Noah," said George coldly, stooping slightly to reach Sinclair's hand.

"Your Majesty," said Sinclair blandly. "May I present my wife, Lady Margaret. . . ."

Margaret curtseyed and George nodded to her. He returned to Sinclair.

"I do hope you'll linger a bit, Sir Noah. Enjoy yourself."

"Inevitably," said Sir Noah.

A hundred feet down the line the chamberlain's memory failed him.

"Your Majesty, may I present—" He stared blankly.

"Inspector Huddleston, Sergeant Pidgeon. How good of you to come."

"Glad to be here," said Huddleston.

"That's right," agreed Pidgeon.

Who the hell are these two? the chamberlain asked himself. And why is that man wearing his overcoat?

George's walk from one end of the room to another took a surprisingly short time—probably a record, thought the chamberlain. The crowd gradually broke ranks, accepting refreshments from servers, first-timers commenting in low voices at the meagerness of the fare. The palace, someone said, likes to handle the massive receptions at £1 a head.

George wheeled quickly among his guests, making, in the chamberlain's opinion, only the vaguest attempt at appearing interested in what people had to say. The chamberlain sighed. He had seen Royal overload before and he would no doubt see it again.

"Ask Captain Stanhope to come here, would you?" asked George of an usher.

Stanhope gently disengaged himself from talking to the wife of the chancellor of the University of Wales and threaded his way through the throng to George.

"Geoffrey," George whispered, "I want you to get hold of the Sinclairs, Astley, my brother, and the two policemen. Show them up to the private wing after I've gone. I want you to join us also."

"Policemen?" asked Stanhope. "What policemen?"

"Their names are Huddleston and Pidgeon. One of them is wearing an overcoat."

"*That* man," said Stanhope. "What is this all about?"

"I have a feeling you know more about it than I do," said George.

Sinclair and Margaret were the last to enter the room. Astley stood by the window, watching the rain begin to fall. Victor Edward shuffled nervously about, thrusting his hands into his pockets and pulling them out again. Huddleston and Pidgeon stood impassively at the doorway, neither quite able to believe he was there.

The room was undistinguished, large and somewhat over-iced with gilt and ormolu. An enormous, shabby painting, dark with dirt, depicted Cochrane's naval victory at the Spanish Roads. George stood still and silent, surveying the room like a schoolmaster waiting for the bell to ring and the class to come to order.

Margaret wheeled Sinclair to the middle of the room, squarely in front of George. Pidgeon closed the door and stood in front of it.

"Now," said George, "I want some answers. Sir Noah, I suggest you begin."

"I failed." Noah shrugged. "We came very close, but we failed. A pity."

"Failed at what?" George demanded.

"This little plan . . ." Sinclair sighed. "Look at this country. It needs a strong king, a man to lead. And instead we have you, a man who does what is expected of him and nothing more. A constitutional monarch. God, how bland."

"Sir Noah is trying to say, sir," said Astley, "that we had hoped that you would abdicate in favor of Prince Edward, leaving the way clear to forming the kind of government that could govern—"

"Gordie—" began Edward apologetically.

"Shut up, Eddie," said George. "You were planning to do what exactly, Sir Noah?"

Sinclair examined his fingernails. "A coup, really. We

170

planned to hang those dirty little crimes on you. You would certainly have been forced to abdicate. You might even have been tried. Edward here would have become King, and we would have taken steps to make sure that Britain had a sporting chance to survive—instead of the slow progress toward destruction that it is pursuing now."

"What exactly did you have in mind?" asked George, a twist of revulsion in his voice.

"Oh," said Sinclair, making a sweeping gesture with his hands, "dissolve Parliament, outlaw the unions—"

"What!" exploded George.

"You see," explained Sinclair patiently, "when I speak of 'we,' I mean more than just the people in this room. You know I have some very influential friends and, I'm pleased to say, they would have backed us. After all, how could they be loyal to a young man who wanders around London murdering tarts?"

"Gordie—" began Edward again.

"You see, your affair with Mrs. Coughlin was really quite perfect. I saw it begin years ago when she was still Jenny Pratt and you were both in my college. When her husband was appointed here, I couldn't help wondering if the old flame had found new life. Imagine my delight when Astley let me know that it had."

"She could have cleared me."

"Ah," said Sinclair, "probably not. . . ."

Pidgeon spoke up. "It's true, sir," he said, as if he were giving evidence. "We picked up a man this morning who had instructions to kill Ambassador and Mrs. Coughlin."

"Make it look like an IRA job," added Huddleston.

"You wretch," said George quietly to Sinclair.

"It was a good plan," said Sinclair. "Much better than just seizing control, don't you think? If we had surrounded the palace with tanks, we would have given the people a martyr. Your stock would have shot up. As a brutal murderer, you would have made us look like the saviors of the nation."

"I don't believe this," said George.

Neither do I, thought Pidgeon.

"Yes," agreed Sinclair, "extraordinary, isn't it? But—I hate to say it—I didn't expect these two gentlemen to be so resourceful. You really put one over on me at Blatchford's, didn't you, Smudge? How does it feel to be a winner? Good, I'll bet, considering your past record. . . ."

But Smudge would not be intimidated. "Well, sir, I think you may have overlooked a few things."

"Did I?" said Sinclair in mock amazement.

"What if I hadn't contacted you? And what were you planning to do about the tape recording we have of the killer's voice?"

"Ah," said Sinclair, as if he were conducting a seminar, "an excellent point. If you hadn't come to me, I would have found my way to you, rest assured. As for the tape, you'll find that it no longer exists. I'm not without friends at the Yard, you know. That's how you two came to be assigned in the first place."

"What do you mean?" demanded Pidgeon.

"You have a very accommodating superior, I understand. A chap named Hartley. I've never spoken to him myself, but my good friend Andrew Drake has dealt with him many times."

"Drake?" said Pidgeon.

"The Permanent Under Secretary of the Home Office."

"Alf was in on this?" said Smudge. He sounded a little hurt.

"No," said Sinclair. " 'Alf' "—he spoke the name as if it had a distinctly unpleasant smell—"was only doing a favor for a superior. He didn't know why, but he didn't ask any questions. He frightens easily, does Alf."

"Why us?" Pidgeon said.

"Dear me," said Sinclair, "you were the obvious choices. Huddleston here has a reputation for doing what he's told. He follows the most obvious leads, plodding along, drawing the most mundane conclusions. We thought we could lead him right to the palace doorstep and, when the time was right, scare him into believing the unbelievable—that the King was a murderer."

Smudge stood stone-faced, his hands clasped in front of him. Looking at him, Pidgeon realized that Sinclair would never, no matter how hard he tried, provoke Smudge into a rash or foolhardy outburst. Smudge was, as he had always been, immovable.

Sinclair shifted in his chair to face Pidgeon. "You, Pidgeon, are a hothead. You would have risked anything to get your man, be he the King of England himself—just what we wanted. We knew that when the last murder occurred you would prove to be too much for Smudge to handle. I just never expected Smudge to defect, to go over to your side. I couldn't imagine old Smudge Huddleston rising up against the hand that had ruled him all these years. . . . I can't think how I overlooked that."

George slumped into a chair. "It revolts me to listen to you."

Margaret shifted uncomfortably. Noah was beginning to get a bit tedious.

"I'm going to have my say while I have the chance," said Sinclair icily. "*You* revolt me. You, of all people, should be doing something for this country, not sitting here while a bunch of cloth-capped yahoos throttle everything we hold dear."

Pidgeon cleared his throat. "Who killed the women?"

Sinclair raised his eyes heavenward. "How prosaic, how policemanlike," he said, as if to himself.

Astley looked up from the window. "A person known to you, sir—a Constable Poole. He said it was difficult in the beginning. But I think he got used to it."

George showed no sign of sadness at Poole's disloyalty. He seemed almost to have expected it.

"Who the hell is Poole?" demanded Pidgeon.

"Really, Sergeant," said Sinclair. "Must we give you all the answers? Poole was Randolph's protégé. . . ."

"He's a member of the palace police," said George weakly. "I trusted him."

"Yes, and while you skulked about Kensington tomcatting, poor Poole had to go do the foul deeds."

"And Geoffrey. How were you involved?"

"Not at all, poor boy," said Sinclair in a patronizing tone of voice. "He was too blinded by what he thought his duty was—rather than what it actually was."

"Gordie—" began Eddie again.

"You don't matter at all," said George.

"Well," said Sinclair, "I think there's nothing more to be said. Shall we go, Margaret?"

"You don't honestly think you're going to walk away from this unpunished, do you?" demanded George.

"Well, yes, actually I do," said Sinclair, as if he were the soul of reason. "To prosecute me would cause an extraordinary scandal. I wouldn't hesitate to tell the whole story. If you think the Blunt affair was embarrassing—" He wheeled himself a foot or so toward the door. "I wouldn't hesitate to name names." He smirked at his self-conscious use of an Americanism. "Shall I tell you some of the names?"

"Yes," said George, "why don't you?"

Sinclair opened his mouth, took a breath, and then stopped himself. "No, I don't think I shall. Suffice it to say that in court I could decimate the government, the armed forces, the Royal Family itself." He nodded at Eddie. "And, besides, I don't imagine you'd like your dirty little liaison with Mrs. Coughlin revealed, would you?"

George stared at the floor. Pidgeon and Huddleston looked around awkwardly.

"No," said Sinclair, "I didn't think so."

EPILOGUE

The Ripper crimes stopped as mysteriously as the first batch had in 1889, and gradually the names of Brenda Pomeroy and Marjorie Stewart faded from memory. The other two victims were never identified. Life returned to normal in Soho, Paddington, and Shepherd Market. The FRENCH MODEL signs began appearing again in dimly lit doorways.

The people soon had a new plaything: a Royal wedding. King George surprised and delighted the nation by announcing his engagement to Lady Alexandra Dunedin ("a superb horsewoman," *Country Life* observed), the fresh-faced if not exactly beautiful daughter of a Scottish lord. Captain Stanhope stood as best man. The Royal couple further enchanted their subjects by producing five children, including three sons, in seven years.

Sir Randolph Astley retired from court life a number of years before he had been expected to, and without the peerage usually awarded to holders of his post. This raised a few eyebrows in court circles, but, as the lord chamberlain observed, "No one ever really liked Randolph."

Prince Victor Edward returned to his regiment, the Royal

Hussars, as did Color Sergeant O'Brian and Regimental Sergeant Major Montague after their long leaves. Both men felt extremely lucky that they had friends in high places.

After a few days in a holding cell, Leary was unceremoniously released, with no further mention of his attempt on the life of the American ambassador. He made straight for the telephone box in Burlington Gardens, where, to his joy, he found the police had forgotten to collect the left-luggage ticket. He claimed the suitcase at Paddington and, locking himself in the public toilet at the station, blew himself to bits. The things that Jones had said he would need in New York turned out to be just over half a pound of gelignite, which detonated when he opened the case. The police report said that Leary was known to have "Irish terrorist connections."

Sir Noah Sinclair achieved great popular acclaim on both sides of the Atlantic with a new book, *The Ripper Revisited*, a witty investigation of the first Jack and the most recent Jack, but not, as Sir Noah pointed out in his introduction, "the last Jack." The book was dedicated "To Margaret, with love" and was filled with patronizing, laudatory references to Huddleston and Pidgeon and their hopeless quest for the new killer.

Hugh Coughlin and Jennifer remained in London for two more years. "He really firmed up his foreign policy overview," Jack Sweeney told friends in Washington. It was a foregone conclusion that Coughlin would run for President—"and win," said Sweeney happily.

Tony Pidgeon seethed about Sinclair for rather a long time. He felt a bit stupid about the way he had been used by Margaret, but he got over it. He left the police force and, to Smudge's surprise, emigrated to Canada. But he was back within a year. He bumped into Harris in a tube station one afternoon and said that he was working for a private security service, looking after the children of Arab sheiks. "He says he hates it," Harris told Hartley.

Constable Poole also left the force. He told his friends that he had come into a bit of money when an aunt died, and opened an attack-dog training school. Business was good.

Smudge Huddleston finished out his months with the force

typing reports and drinking tea. On his retirement, however, his old colleagues were amazed to find that he had been created Samuel Huddleston, OBE, in the Birthday Honors list, "in grateful recognition of services rendered the Crown." Thereafter, Lennie Harris always referred to him as "Sir Smudge."